JAKE'S DRAGON 4

The Conference of Kings

By

RIANO D. MCFARLAND

Vanity Inc.

For Ms. Sue
from
Diana D. McFarland
11/27/2020

Copyright © 2020 by Riano D. McFarland.

All rights reserved. No part of this book may be reproduced or transmitted in any form or by any means, electronic or mechanical, including photocopying, recording, or by an information storage and retrieval system, without permission in writing from the copyright owner.

This is a work of fiction. names, characters, places, and incidents either are the product of the author's imagination or are used fictitiously, and any resemblance to any actual person, living or dead, events, or locales is entirely coincidental.

Any figures depicted in stock imagery are models, and such images are being used for illustrative purposes only.

This novel is dedicated to T'Aer Bolun Dakkar, aka Turbo. Although for many, he would be considered a "rescue" animal, in all honesty, it was he who rescued me. After receiving a cancer diagnosis, I saw him at a local farmers' market outside a tent sponsored by the Animal Foundation of Henderson, Nevada. The moment I laid eyes on him, I knew that we needed each other, and we have been inseparable since the very first time I picked him up. During the pre-surgery preparation, after the surgery, and all through an extended period of recovery requiring nearly 40 radiation therapy sessions, Turbo never left my side. He kept me moving, he made it impossible for me to withdraw from the rest of the world, and no matter how bad I felt or how drained I was, the sound of his whimsical little bark was the music that beat back my post-surgery depression. Three years later, I am cancer-free, and Turbo has gone from a "shelter rescue" to the star depicted on every book cover in the Jake's Dragon series. He has become a beacon of hope for people all over the world. People like me.

CHAPTER 1

THE PATH OF A DRAGON KING is long and arduous. It begins with a full year of captivity inside the thick shell of a ferociously protective female dragon's egg. Dragons lay only odd numbers of eggs, producing broods of between one and seven offspring, depending on the current population of their specific species. During the incubation period, mother dragons remain almost exclusively inside their lairs guarding their precious eggs, leaving them only to gorge themselves on oceanic fish as infrequently as two times per month. Once the hatchlings have slipped from their shells, the mother will leave the lair each night to consume the fish that she will later regurgitate into the mouths of her hungry whelps. Although it takes up to fifty years for a dragon to reach full maturity, within a year, they are quite capable of fending off smaller predators such as foxes, hyenas, dingoes, and domesticated pets like cats and dogs.

Within two years, adolescent dragons, while still incapable of flight, are already excellent swimmers. Even though most are still dependent on the food delivered to the lair by their mothers, those that live along oceanic coastlines or other large bodies of water, are more than willing to follow their mothers into the sea as she hunts for food. At that stage, young dragons lack the skill required to provide for themselves; however, observing the fishing and hunting techniques and tactics of their mothers is an essential part of their development. Since their wings at that stage are not yet fully formed, their hunting excursions are necessarily limited to local bodies of water and their immediate terrestrial surroundings.

Up until a dragon's tenth year, their lives are wholly devoted to sharpening their survival skills, eating massive amounts of fish, and sleeping. The decade that follows, marks a period of puberty in which their physical growth is significantly accelerated. Although still incapable of sustained flight, they are eager to test their wings by gliding from elevated shores and hillsides into the oceans and valleys below them. At this stage, young dragons are already quite fast on both the ground and underwater, and despite their somewhat clumsy appearance, they are also excellent climbers easily scaling large trees and the rocky walls of even the sheerest cliffs.

Dragons are capable of reproducing up to three times during the course of their lives, with females giving birth to, and caring for their young until they are capable of sustained flight, at which time they are weaned from their mothers and able to care for themselves. Until such time, female dragons are fiercely maternal, unwilling to relinquish any part of the parenting process to either their mate or any other dragon for that matter. Although dragon offspring remain tethered to their mothers for a lifetime by an insuppressible tug of familiarity, by the age of twenty-five most dragons are unlikely to ever see their mothers again.

Unlike other dragons, dragon kings will take only one mate during their entire lifetime. While most dragons instinctively seek to mate with another dragon of the same species, if no suitable partner is available, dragons of differing species may mate in order to ensure the preservation of their numbers. In such couplings, the resulting offspring will still be purebred dragons with the females possessing the undiluted DNA of their mothers, and the males possessing that of their fathers with the majority of the brood taking on the identity of the lesser populated dragon species.

Couplings with dragon kings will always produce three eggs, and all of them will be male. A-typically, dragon kings reproduce late in their lifetimes; normally, between eight- and nine-hundred years of age. This allows them ample opportunity to evaluate each of their spawn to determine which of them is most qualified to ascend and assume responsibility of their regional territory. While the first quarter-century of a dragon king's life differs only mildly from that of other dragons, once capable of sustained flight, their lives become akin to a seventy-five year job interview in which their siblings become rivals and their skills, judgement, and experience are all measured against one another until an ascendant king is chosen among them.

Once an ascendant king is chosen, his siblings become his primary lieutenants, assisting the king in the management of their respective global quadrant. Should, for any reason, the appointed king be unable to fulfill his responsibilities, or suffer an untimely demise, the three remaining dragon kings will determine which of the surviving lieutenants ascend to replace him.

As the eldest of the regional dragon kings, King J'Amal Aidin Kondur's reign over the Northeastern Dragon Kingdom was approaching its end. He and the legendary King Tao Min Xiong had ascended during the same era, and while he unquestionably commanded the respect of all other dragons and dragon kings, having outlived both of his senior lieutenants, the time had come to evaluate the descendants of his royal lineage and select a dragon king ascendant who would succeed him.

T'Pal, Mi'Kael, and J'Mir Mahajan were the three, perfect offspring of a beautiful Indian Naga Dragoness named Sirina Mahajan. Her lineage was ancient even by dragon standards, and the genetic memories she passed on to her children pre-dated even those of the Southwestern Dragon King, Sha'Kaa Santiago. While each of her whelps were similar in stature and appearance, their characters varied in a number of ways with each possessing strengths and weaknesses that required extensive vetting prior to ascending to the throne of King J'Amal Aidin Kondur.

As is often the case with siblings, T'Pal, Mi'Kael, and J'Mir were in a constant state of rivalry that influenced their every undertaking. Each feeding venture was a competition, each flight was a race, and the dreamscape battles waged between the three young bulls were of unprecedented intensity among dragons of their age and level of maturity, often lasting for days on end. Even as King J'Amal Aidin Kondur closely followed their evolution, he did not interfere, realizing his intervention could have a dampening effect on the arc of their individual development.

There is no standardized test to evaluate the worthiness of potential dragon king ascendants. No written examination could even scratch the surface of the traits required to successfully rule a regional dragon kingdom. Dragons have survived for millions of years by adapting to the ever-changing social and environmental conditions surrounding them, and since the formation of their loose alliance with humans, those conditions were often fluid at best, and unstable at worst. Nevertheless, in order to ensure peaceful cohabitation among Earth's two dominant species, concessions were required of both humans and dragons in order to avoid potentially cataclysmic confrontations that could escalate beyond the ability of either side to contain them.

Despite the genetically inherited history bestowed upon dragon offspring by their mothers, the wisdom associated with that knowledge was not always immediately apparent. In fact, there is occasionally a deep chasm between the awareness of one's history and the wisdom to be derived from it. As with humans, young dragons are often impulsive and defiant, and while their innate curiosity can be the catalyst that leads to advancements within their civilizations, failing to carefully consider the causes and effects of their actions could potentially produce catastrophic results. Even knowledge genetically passed down through a thousand generations is occasionally subject to individual interpretation and adaptation to changing times and public sentiment. These differing interpretations are also possible among identical dragon triplets.

Admittedly, there are benefits to be gleaned from the experience of sibling rivalries; however, ultimately an ascendant dragon king must be able to stand on his own merits, and behind his decisions even when those decisions are flawed.

Before reaching the end of his incubation period, King T'Aer Bolun Dakkar had been robbed of his siblings, and thrust into a situation requiring him to care and provide for a mother who had been mortally wounded while trying to retrieve two of her eggs from an armada of power-thirsty dragoneers. Although she'd been unable to save her babies who perished without ever emerging from their shells, the crew of the armada that had stolen them soon joined them in their eternal slumber on the floor of the icy North Atlantic Ocean.

While admittedly benefitting from the undivided attention received as the only surviving offspring of Sahar Talin Dakkar, T'Aer Bolun Dakkar spent the majority of his first century in relative isolation, unaware of the multiple layers of protection afforded him by his father, Tao Min Xiong, following the premature loss of his mother. Only after meeting the eleven-year-old boy who would become his bonded rider, did T'Aer Bolun Dakkar come to realize the importance of mutually shared development and the benefits of having a confidant to whom he could impart his bounty of knowledge.

As T'Pal, Mi'Kael, and J'Mir Mahajan ushered in the anniversary of their first completed century, the evaluation of their knowledge, skills, and their wisdom in applying them would be tested on a level well beyond anything either of them had ever faced. In stark contrast to the three-quarter-century period of passive observation they'd undergone, their final evaluation phase would be conducted under close scrutiny of the Conference of Kings J'Amal Aidin Kondur of the Northeastern Dragon Kingdom, Kai Bok Katari of the Southeastern Dragon Kingdom, Sha'Kaa Santiago of the Southwestern Dragon Kingdom, and the King of Kings T'Aer Bolun Dakkar from the Northwestern Dragon Kingdom. Having inherited knowledge of the existence of each dragon king from their mother, Sirina Mahajan, each of the three candidates were anxious to apply the skills they had acquired in real world situations both inside and outside the realm of Ahl Sha H'Araah.

    Still... Knowing of a dragon king's existence by way of genetically inherited memories is one thing; however, standing face-to-face with them is quite another, especially when one of them happens to be Jake's Dragon.

CHAPTER 2

IT HAD BEEN NEARLY FIVE YEARS since the last assembly of dragon kings, following the departure of the Drokarians. While their incessant monitoring of Earth's interconnected biosphere was a never-ending endeavor, the balance within their respective regions were on undeniable trajectories of improvement. Thanks to the cutting-edge techniques and uniquely tailored solutions developed by Jake and Danni through application of the knowledge obtained from the Drokarian scientists, many areas once considered unsalvageable were now well along their roads to recovery. With three of the four dragon realms now vigorously represented by bonded riders, deviations from their specified course correction measures could be immediately identified and quickly addressed.

When the call for assembly was received inside the unspoiled dimension of Nin'Jahlah, the sprawling Columbian farmlands near Bogota, and the now pristine waters near Adelaide in South Australia, three dragon kings took flight with their bonded riders, converging on the location of the Northeastern Dragon King's lair. In the snow-covered expanse of the Himalayas, they were all warmly welcomed into the frozen realm of King J'Amal Aidin Kondur.

"Greetings, great kings and valiant warriors," said J'Amal Aidin Kondur. Foregoing all idle small-talk, he announced, "My reign as king is approaching its end. While it has been an honor to live and rule among the greatest collection of dragon kings since the beginning of time, and to witness the ascension of each of you, I must now select the most capable of my descendants to take up the reigns of leadership and join your ranks as king of the Northeastern

Dragon Kingdom. Having languished in the presence of such iconic kings as D'Nal Rafcm and the legendary Tao Min Xiong, it is now incumbent upon me to choose as wisely as they have chosen. In order to ensure this appointment is based upon merit rather than emotion, I seek your counsel and guidance in making that decision."

Looking in the direction of the King of Kings, he said, "King T'Aer Bolun Dakkar, I ask your permission to convene a Conference of Kings over which you would preside. While each of us will choose the manner and means in which our own individual challenges are presented, it will be you who objectively evaluates the results before making your recommendation. The final challenge will be presented by you and evaluated by the three remaining dragon kings until a consensus has been reached."

Nodding in agreement, T'Aer Bolun Dakkar said, "Jake and I accept your appointment and pledge to offer our unbiased conclusions and an objective recommendation."

"As will we," stated Kai Bok Katari with the agreement of his bonded rider, Svend Erickson.

"And we," replied Sha'Kaa Santiago signaling the consent of both himself and Sibyl Dupree.

"Very well," said King J'Amal Aidin Kondur. "It is with the utmost gratitude that I welcome your participation. The conference will convene thirty days from now, and the order of the challenges shall be determined by King T'Aer Bolun Dakkar. I will inform each contestant without delay and make formal introductions prior to commencement of the challenges."

Having silently reached an unspoken accord, the three visiting dragon kings disappeared into the moonless night sky above the Himalayan mountain range. Moments later, King J'Amal Aidin Kondur emitted the tug of familiarity, summoning T'Pal, Mi'Kael, and J'Mir Mahajan, to the location vacated by the assembly of dragon kings, only minutes prior to their near simultaneous arrival.

T'Pal was the first to arrive, landing and rearing onto his hind legs while extending his wings out to the sides. His formal greeting posture was mirrored by his father and repeated with the subsequent arrivals of J'Mir and Mi'Kael as he welcomed them to his secluded Tibetan lair.

As the eldest, even if only by a few minutes, T'Pal was the most reserved of the three dragon siblings. His cautious nature was reflected in his somber countenance and his tendency to over-think situations in which expedience would have been warranted. While of the three dragons, T'Pal was the least likely to rush blindly into an ill-considered predicament, a dragon king does not always have the luxury of time when facing life or death decisions. Left to his own devices, T'Pal would routinely err on the side of caution, making his actions highly predictable.

By comparison, Mi'Kael emerged from his protective shell only minutes behind T'Pal; however, their personalities could not have been more divergent. Mi'Kael was a veritable fountain of good intentions, but rarely if ever has a dragon been more easily distracted. In situations untethered to time constraints, Mi'Kael was able to produce results that were the equivalent of artistic masterpieces. Unfortunately, when facing stressful decisions and a ticking timeclock, he was often overwhelmed and unable to rise to the occasion.

As the last of the hatchlings to emerge, J'Mir was a natural diplomat, always hoping to find mutually acceptable means to arrive at pre-determined ends. What he possessed in terms of negotiation skills, he lacked in his ability to personally execute and implement the negotiated terms. At times, J'Mir seemed more interested in winning the intellectual debates than he was in solving the problems that sparked them. While intellectual dexterity is a highly admirable trait, dragon kings must be able to perceive and implement just decisions, even when those decisions are unpopular.

Without regard to their strengths and weaknesses, each of his offspring were a source of great pride for King J'Amal Aidin Kondur. He was convinced that each of them would be excellent dragon kings, making it impossible for him to arrive at an objective decision regarding which of them should assume the reins of power upon his passing. The Conference of Kings would provide an objective format in which each of their strengths and weaknesses could be tested and evaluated by a panel of trusted kings and bonded riders. Unlike J'Amal Aidin Kondur, their judgement would be fair, balanced, and objectively delivered, based on the individual performances of each contestant during their evaluations.

While the Northeastern Dragon King had been keeping tabs on them since they were weaned, after departing their birth lair, their only contacts to each other had been inside the dreamscape scenarios designed by King J'Amal Aidin Kondur. Despite their decades-long separation, the three brothers were thrilled at the unexpected reunion, and vowed to support the new dragon king ascendant, no matter which of them were ultimately selected.

Upon receiving the blessings and well wishes of the father they had all just met for the first time that very evening, the three would-be dragon kings disappeared into the night sky, parting ways to begin preparations for the Conference of Kings. J'Amal Aidin Kondur's gaze followed each of them as they melded with the starlit sky above. Satisfied with the events of the day, he turned and walked into the snowy expanse, quickly vanishing among the anonymous peaks of the frozen Himalayas.

In what might seem to be a counterintuitive aspect of the Conference of Kings, at no time would the three dragon siblings participate in direct competition with one another. In fact, pending the final determination of the assembly of dragon kings, T'Pal, Mi'Kael, and J'Mir would not even be permitted to communicate with each other, in order to preserve the absolute integrity of the contested evaluations. Most areas of appraisal were designed to test a dragon king's problem-solving abilities, placing higher emphasis on the effectiveness of the solution, rather than on the speed at which it was achieved. Although the evaluations would not include "trick" questions, there could in fact, be several correct answers to the same question.

By soliciting the active participation of all dragon kings, King J'Amal Aidin Kondur had already proven the depth of his understanding, firmly cementing into place the cornerstone of his legacy as a wise and just king. As the remaining territorial leaders prepared for their roles in the Conference of Kings, there were arrangements to be made, questions to be formulated, and obstacles to be designed that would challenge the physical prowess, intellectual maturity, wisdom, and loyalty of each highly-qualified contestant. Each of them possessed fountains of knowledge and experience to draw from in determining the essential traits of a dragon king.

When it came to loyalty, there was none more proven than Svend Erickson who, despite multiple incarcerations and a twenty-year forced separation from his beloved King Kai Bok Katari, never revealed even the slightest of details regarding the secrets of the dragon realm. Even in exile, his loyalty and dedication to his bonded dragon did not waiver.

The dogged determination and archeological expertise of Sibyl Dupree made her an authority on a multitude of Earth's ancient civilizations. She was as cunning and clever as the black wolf with whom she eagerly patrolled the deepest regions of the Amazon Rainforest. Whether sprinting alongside King Sha'Kaa Santiago through the thickest of South American jungles or soaring above the magnificent Andes astride him as her bonded dragon, their joint tenacity made them both formidable opponents and treasured allies.

For well over a decade, Jacob Payne had been the planet's only bonded rider, tirelessly pursuing the environmental balance that ensured the survival of our world's multiple ecosystems while preventing the territorial conflicts that would otherwise have pitted its two dominant species at odds with one another. With the aid of his wife, Danni, and Bonded to King T'Aer Bolun Dakkar—the most powerful dragon king in Earth's four billion year history—even a billion dollar bounty on their heads could not derail their crusade to save the planet, and reverse the downward spiral of its ecosystems.

Under the wisdom and guidance of King T'Aer Bolun Dakkar, this Conference of Kings would yield a fair and impartial result and reveal a dragon king ascendant worthy of ruling the Northeastern Dragon Kingdom.

CHAPTER 3

"HOW DOES ONE EVALUATE the qualifications of a dragon king ascendant?" asked Jake. "There is no single factor or even group of factors I can imagine that could prepare anyone to assume such a role. We've gone from dragoneers to Drokarians in fewer than twenty years, and a dragon king will rule for a thousand. Who knows what will happen during such an expansive period?"

"The responsibilities of a dragon king are not defined in a set of golden rules," replied T'Aer Bolun Dakkar. "The challenges that arise will be fluid and unpredictable, and an effective dragon king must be wise and open-minded in order to meet those challenges."

"Since your ascension, I cannot even count the number of unexpected plot twists we've encountered," said Jake with a smile. "For a while, it seemed we would both collapse from sheer exhaustion. Fortunately, Svend and Sibyl have been extremely effective at marshalling their resources and representing their regions."

"Because of the work done by you and Danni, King J'Amal Aidin Kondur and the Northeastern Dragon Kingdom are actually well-positioned to confront any issues requiring an elevated level of engagement," said T'Aer Bolun Dakkar. "The pride the Northeastern Dragon King holds for his three heirs is also well founded. Although their characters differ greatly, their love and concern for both the dragon and human populations of their region, are verifiable and sincere."

"They have certainly had an excellent role model to pattern themselves after," stated Jake. "King J'Amal Aidin Kondur's leadership has been impeccable, and his distinguished presence will most certainly be missed, regardless of which son replaces him."

As Jake and T'Aer Bolun Dakkar crossed the void of Ahl Sha H'Araah into Nin'Jahlah, their mere presence in the realm always elicited the same reaction from the tribe. By the time they landed, their entire family of hybrid dinosaurs had gathered in anticipation of showering them with affection, which each time, they graciously received and reciprocated.

Upon dismounting, Jake immediately relieved Tikka of the dimension's two newest residents; Sammy and Jewel Payne. The fraternal twins had arrived almost four years earlier, ending the speculation as to whether Jake's and Danni's first born would be a boy or a girl. The surprise could not have been more welcome to Big Sam and Sarah, and Richard and Julia Hawthorne; all of whom had grown increasingly impatient, longing for grandchildren. The joy surrounding their arrival had been just as warmly received by their family in Tennessee as it was by the tribe in Nin'Jahlah. Having given birth to them in Nashville, Danni remained there with her family for the first few months so the grandparents on both sides of the family could spoil them rotten under the guise of helping Danni take care of them.

For Sammy and Jewel, the love for their human family members was no different than that for Tikka and the tribe, who seemed utterly enthralled by them. When Tikka saw the twins, it was love at first sight. Even wrapped inside their individual pink and blue blankets, she felt the immediate yearning to protect them. As they grew, she was able to decipher the unintelligible coos and gurgles uttered by them even before they could speak. While Sammy's first spoken word was "Mama," Jewel's first word was "Tikka," and aside from their usual clucks and baby noises, they also appeared to have developed a language only the two of them could understand.

Whether dressed in matching toddler-sized overalls and dashing along the aisles inside Big Sam's shop, or romping through the lush greenery of Nin'Jahlah in their birthday suits with a cadre of hybrid dinosaurs carefully monitoring their every step, Sammy and Jewel were happy and loved beyond all measure. Danni and Jake would often watch with amazement as the two of them darted playfully through a grassy meadow with the tribe following them in a manner reminiscent of a children's soccer team, following the ball in a concentrated swarm, regardless of who was in possession of it.

The concern that they could inadvertently be trampled or injured by one of the two-ton dinosaurs around them quickly dissipated like the tendrils of smoke from an extinguished candle wick. Once, while chasing a large blue butterfly through the open field, Jewel tripped over a small twig laying in the grass. She was more shocked than injured but began to cry. Tikka seemed mortified, and the tenderness with which she helped Jewel to her feet was breathtaking. After inspecting his little sister, Sammy brushed the grass from her padded little toddler knees and moments later, they were holding hands and in pursuit of the butterfly again, as if nothing had even happened. Later that afternoon while the children were napping, Tikka and the tribe removed every single piece of debris from the field, leaving nothing even remotely large enough for the twins to stumble over and fall again.

One morning, after the first daily fish haul with the trebuchet, Sammy and Jewel discovered that they could use the stone ramp to climb onto the backs of the dinosaurs. After that morning, the tribe of dinosaurs literally took turns giving the twins rides around the meadow!

As unimaginable as this may have seemed to anyone living outside the realm of Nin'Jahlah, for the twins, it was as normal as riding the tractor-tire swing, hanging from the tree in Grandpa Sam's back yard. All things considered; the twins were well-adjusted despite the highly contrasting worlds in which they lived.

They could also immediately sense the excitement of the tribe when Jake and T'Aer Bolun Dakkar returned to Nin'Jahlah and were just as anxious to greet them as were their family of hybrid dinosaurs. Danni would watch from their modest home in the distance as Tikka taxied the twins down the hillside to T'Aer Bolun Dakkar's customary landing zone. One after another, they would leap from Tikka's back into the embrace of a loving father who could not wait to get his arms around them.

At that precise moment, King J'Amal Aidin Kondur's predicament zoomed clearly into focus as Jake's adoring children clung to him like baby sugar gliders. Even if it were required of him, Jake would most definitely not be able to choose one of his children over the other for such a monumental appointment. As the weight of reality settled upon his shoulders, he felt fortunate to have been spared that particular aspect of a dragon king's responsibilities.

Nevertheless, during the next thirty days, he, and King T'Aer Bolun Dakkar would endeavor to create a challenge worthy of a dragon king ascendant. This same responsibility would be incumbent upon the remaining dragon kings; however, the King of Kings would also hold the scales of measurement by which the next Northeastern Dragon King would be selected. It was a process that would not be concocted in haste.

"Out there, saving the world without me again?" asked Danni from the porch as Jake climbed the steps with his precious cargo.

"*For* you. Not *without* you," Jake replied, finally setting Sammy and Jewel down to make room for the arrow through his heart. Danni immediately filled the void left by the kids, tiptoeing to kiss him while reflexively lifting her left leg behind her.

As the children ran into the house to wash their hands and faces before dinner, Jake told Danni, "King J'Amal Aidin Kondur will be selecting his ascendant soon."

Following somewhat of a stunned silence, Danni asked, "How soon?"

"The selection process will begin one month from now," replied Jake. "Once the ascendant has been chosen, there will be a short transition period after which, King J'Amal Aidin Kondur will relinquish reign of his region to the new king."

Years earlier, Danni spent several months in Tokyo working on the renewable energy project that revolutionized the automobile industry. Although her very presence there was viewed as a threat by most of the world's automotive manufacturing giants, King J'Amal Aidin Kondur's presence was like an impenetrable dome of protection for her. Despite the dozens of threats leveled at Takai Motor Company and at her personally, she did not sense even a hint of danger once Jake informed her King J'Amal Aidin Kondur had personally guaranteed her safety. She never saw him but the absolute lack of interference during her work there, was clearly not attributable to coincidence.

"He's been an excellent dragon king," said Danni. "I'm sure his wisdom will carry on, even after passing the mantle of responsibility."

Jake, Danni, and the twins enjoyed dinner together as the Nin'Jahlan sun began to set. Outside near the water's edge, the tribe was busy consuming their last haul of fish for the day under the watchful eyes of King T'Aer Bolun Dakkar. In a process that had been repeated thousands of times during the evolutionary course of dragons, the transition of dragon kings was almost always fraught with pitfalls. The amount of power and influence that comes with a dragon's ascension to king were not to be underestimated.

Having had no siblings, for nearly a quarter-century, T'Aer Bolun Dakkar had defended his right to ascend against dozens of challengers away from the eyes of humans, inside the realm of Ahl Sha H'Araah. These battles were against dragons from both inside and outside the Northwestern Dragon Kingdom. His uniqueness within the dragon realm gave rise to an upheaval of epic proportions. Although a dragon king is only challengeable during the first one hundred years of his rule, those challenges can come from anywhere across all dragon kingdoms. In T'Aer Bolun Dakkar's case, the challenges began shortly after his mother departed for the ancestral burial chamber in the Northwestern Dragon Kingdom.

At merely twenty-five years of age, T'Aer Bolun Dakkar began defending his right to ascend against a veritable onslaught of self-proclaimed dragon king ascendants. Had he been bested by any one of them, the throne of King Tao Min Xiong would have effectively been up for grabs. Without siblings to defend the royal blood line, defeating T'Aer Bolun Dakkar would have resulted in legal anarchy, with the right to rule going to the victor, regardless of their species, origin, or lineage. Instead of having to defeat three of Tao Min Xiong's offspring, challengers would only need to defeat one, giving them much better odds at securing the throne for themselves.

Despite odds which were stacked terribly against him, T'Aer Bolun Dakkar accepted all challengers while fighting for his blood inheritance. There were hundreds of them, and as they hoped for an opportunity to strike at a moment of vulnerability due to physical exhaustion, emotional fatigue, or a forced or unforced error on his part, T'Aer Bolun Dakkar remained undefeated against all who stood before him. With each ensuing battle, he became stronger, faster, wiser, and infinitely more skilled in dispatching his opponents. By the time he chose Jake and began engaging in dreamscape battles with him, there were no dragons remaining who would dare to openly challenge him.

Although King J'Amal Aidin Kondur's three offspring possessed the knowledge and wisdom of their father through the inherited genetic memories of their mother, Sirina Mahajan, what they did not possess was the royal bloodline of an ancestral dragon king. The Northeastern Dragon King, NaDahl D'Monicus had forfeited his claim to the throne after unsuccessfully challenging King Tao Min Xiong. As the victor, King Tao Min Xiong had won the right to rule Earth's entire northern hemisphere. Instead, he selected J'Amal Aidin Kondur to serve as king, and once installed

King Tao Min Xiong fully respected the autonomy of the northeastern region, never again interfering in their regional affairs.

Unlike T'Aer Bolun Dakkar, NaDahl D'Monicus had siblings; one of whom had been biding his time, preparing for the day when King J'Amal Aidin Kondur would relinquish the Northeastern Dragon Kingdom to an ascendant. As a blood descendant of King Satir D'Monicus, Bokur D'Monicus chose an existence cloaked in obscurity. He and J'Amal Aidin Kondur were of the same age, and when the Northeastern Dragon King took a mate, so did Bokur D'Monicus, assuring that his offspring would also be of the appropriate age when it was time to select an ascendant dragon king.

Now that word of the upcoming Conference of Kings was spreading throughout the Northeastern Dragon Kingdom, Bokur D'Monicus planned on seizing the moment to return reign of that region back to the true royal bloodline, and like J'Amal Aidin Kondur... Bokur D'Monicus *also* had three sons.

CHAPTER 4

XIANA SAFIR WAS AMBITIOUS far beyond the boundaries of tradition in the Northeastern Dragon Kingdom. She had no preference for the dragon species she would choose as a mate, as long as he was a dragon king. Unlike Sirina Mahajan, Xiana Safir had no intention of disappearing into the shadows should one of her offspring ascend to the throne of King J'Amal Aidin Kondur. As a Hydra Dragoness, Xiana Safir was a six-headed cauldron of trouble and deceit. She had openly courted King J'Amal Aidin Kondur as a mate, offering to bear his offspring; however, he intuitively recognized her ulterior motives and chose instead to mate with the Naga Dragoness.

Despite the obviousness of her own deceitful intentions, she feigned outrage at being rejected and sought to take her revenge by forming an alliance with Bokur D'Monicus. Now, she would bear *his* offspring and assist him in dismantling the current hierarchy of the Northeastern Dragon Kingdom, in return for an elevated status as honorary queen and co-ruler of the region. For her, this seemed only fitting as the next king would surely be one of her own children. Due to dragons' genetically inherited deference to their mothers, even as dragon king, he would be unable to resist her demands, giving her de facto authority over the entire northeastern realm.

As king, J'Amal Aidin Kondur was bound by dragon law to accept all challengers vying for the right to ascend to his throne. Since the D'Monicus bloodline was verifiably of royal descent, they were not even required to seek the permission of the current dragon king once the Conference of Kings was announced. They need only state their intention to participate, which they did within hours of the official proclamation by King J'Amal Aidin Kondur.

In accordance with the terms of the conference, he notified the remaining dragon kings of the additions to the roster of challengers. Due to the extraordinary rarity of circumstances surrounding this specific dragon kingdom, the list of prospective dragon king ascendants continued to grow.

Customarily, dragon kings of royal lineage will appoint one of their own offspring as dragon king ascendant, foregoing the process of an open competition. However, since J'Amal Aidin Kondur was a first-generation dragon king by proclamation, the royal lineage could only be considered as established if one of his offspring ascended to the throne. It had been nearly a thousand generations since the last Conference of Kings was convened, and with the throne open for challengers from kingdoms around the globe, the roster would with absolute certainty expand even further.

Despite the realization that a conference would dramatically increase the field of competition, King J'Amal Aidin Kondur had full confidence in his three sons and sought to avoid any perceived conflicts of interest that could undermine the legitimacy of the chosen dragon king ascendant. Independent of his own children, it was his desire to select the dragon best suited to the responsibility of leading the Northeastern Dragon Kingdom into the coming millennium. With King T'Aer Bolun Dakkar serving as conference chairman, the impartiality of the selection process was assured.

In the sanctity of her secluded lair, midway between Sri Lanka and Malaysia in the deep black waters of the Indian Ocean, Xiana Safir and her mate, Bokur D'Monicus were already considering strategies to quickly thin the herd between their three spawn and the throne of the Northeastern Dragon Kingdom. While most of them would not even make it past the king's avatars during battles inside the realm of Ahl Sha H'Araah, those who did would go on to face challenges from the three remaining dragon kings. Even though their challenges would remain confidential until the opening day of the Conference of Kings, they were designed to separate the unworthy from the determined by exploiting weaknesses, undermining self-confidence, and eliminating even the possibility of beginners luck as a deciding factor. The challenges would be difficult. In fact, they would be *exceedingly* difficult even for those with the genetically inherited knowledge of a dragon king, and his royal blood coursing through their veins. There was still one week remaining before the conference convened, and the roster already bore the names of some twenty challengers.

With greed and an unquenchable thirst for power energizing them, Xiana Safir and Bokur D'Monicus would stop at nothing to derail the hopes of as many challengers as they could, weakening them and diminishing their chances of success whenever and wherever possible.

All of this would be of little or no surprise among the challengers populating the roster. In fact, they expected it. The boundaries of each dragon king's challenge scenarios were as broad as the planet itself. Fair play was not even in the terminology of such a competition, and although Xiana Safir and Bokur D'Monicus were collaborating in secret, this was only to prevent other challengers from discovering their strategies and tactics and developing measures to counter them.

Truthfully, a Conference of Kings is an invitation to charlatans, frauds, swindlers, and opportunists. It is akin to walking barefoot through a teeming pit of vipers and scorpions, while attempting to count to a million with your hair on fire. In short, it is designed to make challengers fail, and fail miserably.

Like humans, the dragon civilization is populated by individuals with varying agendas. They seek to secure territorial advantages which benefit not only themselves, but also their descendants. Despite a total population of fewer than four hundred dragons worldwide, due to their natural longevity, their actions on any given day could potentially affect millions of others along family bloodlines. An effective dragon king will seek equity among the clans of their region, while maintaining the critical balance necessary to prevent dragon rivalries from spilling over into the realm of humans. Even after their successful alliance in countering the Drokarian threat, it was vitally important to maintain the veil of separation between dragon and human societies. This was every dragon king's primary objective.

As king of all dragon kings, T'Aer Bolun Dakkar puzzled deeply over the upcoming Conference of Kings, perhaps even more so than the other dragon kings. Once a new ascendant was selected, it was his duty, along with J'Amal Aidin Kondur, to prepare them for the enormous responsibility they would assume. Having received the scenarios from the other dragon kings, he had already determined the order of the challenges.

First, King J'Amal Aidin Kondur would evaluate each challenger's physical and tactical battle skills inside the realm of Ahl Sha H'Araah. The avatars the challengers would face were nearly impossible to defeat, having at most, a single vulnerability that must be discovered and successfully exploited in order to emerge victorious. There was no time limit, and the battle would continue until either the dragon or the king's avatar was defeated.

Those who emerged victorious from the first challenge would then face King Sha'Kaa Santiago and his bonded rider, Sibyl Dupree. Each challenger would select an avatar in the form of which, they would compete in a flag challenge. A specific location would be identified only moments before the start of the hunt and using only their genetically inherited memories, challengers must locate and capture the flag before King Sha'Kaa Santiago and his bonded rider secured it. Each challenger could only choose a single avatar that would become their permanent representative among the world of humans should they succeed. Failing to secure the flag would not automatically result in the challenger's elimination. If everyone failed, everyone advanced to the next challenge;

however, if even a single challenger succeeded in securing the flag, all those who did not, were eliminated.

At the conclusion of the flag competition, challengers would face King Kai Bok Katari and Svend Erickson in the ivory challenge. Their event would take place wholly inside the realm of Ahl Sha H'Araah in an area encompassing Africa, the Indian Ocean, and Australia. The task was relatively simple. Locate two ivory tusks in Africa and deliver them to Melbourne. While the task itself, seemed almost too easy, there were unspecified metrics by which each challenger would be measured, and they would remain secret until the winner was declared.

Finally, any competitor who completed the gamut of challenges from the other three regional dragon kings, would face King T'Aer Bolun Dakkar to answer one single question. The same question would be asked of each prospective dragon king ascendant; however, the correct answer would remain the solitary secret of King T'Aer Bolun Dakkar until he revealed it at the end of the Conference of Kings.

With the order of the challenges set and the roster of challengers expanding with each passing day, this Conference of Kings was certain to be epic in its size and scope. There would be those who would seek to cover their own skill deficits by attempting to compromise the abilities of others. Hidden among noble dragons, there would be connivers who believed themselves capable of deceiving their opponents and wresting victory away from a dragon infinitely more suited to the duties of a dragon king.

On the other hand, there would be noble, valiant dragons from across all of Earth's dragon kingdoms, hoping to underscore and perpetuate the work and accomplishments of King J'Amal Aidin Kondur and secure his legacy for generations to come. Even dragons who entered the competition with selfish agendas in mind, often exited it with a much broader understanding of a dragon king's responsibilities and a greater sense of respect for the dragon chosen to ascend. Regardless of each dragon's reason for entering the fray, the champion who emerged victorious would undoubtedly be well-suited for ascension to the throne of King J'Amal Aidin Kondur.

With the parameters of the competition in place and the beginning of the conference mere hours away, King T'Aer Bolun Dakkar felt a sense of pageantry for the competition that would determine the course of the Northeastern Dragon Kingdom for a thousand years to come. Staring out across the unspoiled waters of the Nin'Jahlan Sea, he realized that he and Jake were now ready to dispatch their roles with the honor and integrity due such an all-encompassing event.

Smiling while observing the pride of beautiful hybrid dinosaurs populating the field separating them, he said to Jake, "Let the conference begin."

CHAPTER 5

BOTH BOKUR D'MONICUS AND XIANA SAFIR were anxious for the Conference of Kings to commence. Although they seemed quite confident in their offspring's abilities, there was no evidentiary foundation upon which to base their optimism. Neither the order nor the nature of the challenges had yet been revealed by T'Aer Bolun Dakkar, and while the other dragon kings had presented their individual challenge scenarios to him, beyond their own submissions, not even *they* knew the order or the full nature of the competition structure.

Female dragons name their young according to their own traditions and those of their mate. Some will include elements of the father's name and others will not. In the D'Monicus bloodline, all male dragons bore the D'Monicus name without exception. Accordingly, Mi'Kah, K'Zahn, and Na'Desh were all intent on reviving and restoring the D'Monicus name to its former glory. With the treachery of their ancestors Satir and NaDahl D'Monicus casting shadows along their ancestral bloodline, their genetically inherited memories were a constant reminder of their disgraced family name. Should one of the D'Monicus challengers emerge victorious as the dragon king ascendant, both siblings would become his primary lieutenants and the D'Monicus name would once again be respected throughout the Northeastern Dragon Kingdom.

Unlike most dragons, particularly dragon kings, Mi'Kah, K'Zahn, and Na'Desh were never truly weaned from Xiana Safir. She had carefully plotted a course to keep them within her sphere of influence in anticipation of the vacancy left by King J'Amal Aidin

Kondur. In the world of humans, a century might seem an extraordinarily long period of time; however, for dragons who routinely live for more than three-hundred years, the reward of potentially exercising her influence over a dragon king for a hundred years or more, was well worth the sacrifice. Of course, there was that pesky little matter of the Conference of Kings, and two-dozen others who were just as convinced that *they* would emerge victorious.

Granted, there were only a handful possessing the genetically inherited memories of dragon kings, but some of them were the descendants of great warriors like Se'Thaa Malka'Am who, with a single flight, ushered in the end of the Cretaceous Period and the extinction of the dinosaurs. Still, Xiana Safir's prediction that most would not advance beyond the battle arena where they would face King J'Amal Aidin Kondur's avatars, was more likely than unlikely. Even the current king's offspring were in no way guaranteed success during that challenge.

To facilitate reckless overconfidence among most of the challengers, Xiana Safir initiated a propaganda campaign that led many of them to believe there would be an hour-long journey into the heart of Ahl Sha H'Araah before the avatar would engage them. She posited that it would fatigue each dragon prior to their actual battle, lowering their level of endurance and dulling their reflexes to a point that made them less effective in confronting the king's avatar. Whether or not this information was accurate, had yet to be proven; however, even as an unsubstantiated rumor, it crept stealthily into the subconscious of the contenders like poisonous oleander oil. Needless to say; her offspring would be ready to engage an adversary the instant they crossed the trans-dimensional rift into Ahl Sha H'Araah.

Although this misinformation campaign would certainly not influence every challenger, perhaps it would sow seeds of over-confidence in some of them, and fear of failure in others who lacked the endurance to engage a foe after such a lengthy flight into the battle zone. The training and preparation of young dragon kings begins even before they can fly, and they are perpetually ready for engagement. Accordingly, propaganda and misinformation have little to no effect on their state of preparedness, as they are *always* deadly adversaries.

Neither Bokur D'Monicus nor Xiana Safir had knowledge of the other challenges the contenders would face, but there was always a test of battle worthiness. It was certainly safe to surmise it would be intense and that no quarter would be given. During this Conference of Kings, it was one of only two challenges by which contenders would be eliminated if defeated, unless *all* of them were defeated. Obviously, if there were one challenge upon which to concentrate their energies, the battle challenge would provide the biggest return on their invested time.

The night before commencement of the Conference of Kings, Earth's skies were void of dragons with the sole exception of the King of Kings, T'Aer Bolun Dakkar. All other dragons withdrew to their secluded lairs and roosts, where they slept from midnight to midnight, channeling their energy and emotional support to their champion of choice. This was an important ritual throughout all of Earth's dragon kingdoms. In the same manner by which related dragons exerted their tug of familiarity, they were also able to funnel energy to their preferred dragon king ascendant, much in the same manner as humans do when voting during elections. For a contender to the regional throne, the energy they received was detectable, and it could be utilized to augment their own energy during the competition. Unlike in human elections, this energy could not be diverted or corrupted; therefore, the outcome more accurately reflected the consensus of the dragon realm as a collective, by proportionately amplifying the power of the champion they have chosen to represent them.

During the period of "Dragon Sleep", Jake and T'Aer Bolun Dakkar patrolled the skies of all dragon kingdoms, protecting the entirety of the dragon realm that bequeathed their *own* valuable energy to the seven chakras of another as they slept.

"It is so peaceful in the skies tonight," said Jake. "I never imagined the subtle pulses emitted by other dragons could be so obvious in their absence."

"The Dragon Sleep is a seldom-experienced occurrence," replied T'Aer Bolun Dakkar. "I know of it only through my genetic ancestral memories, yet even they fall short in comparison to the pronounced absence of them in reality."

"I am still amazed at the number of contenders who have presented themselves for the conference," said Jake. "More than anything, I am impressed that King J'Amal Aidin Kondur has so wholly embraced this competition."

"King J'Amal Aidin Kondur is a just and noble ruler," said T'Aer Bolun Dakkar. "He seeks to identify the best dragon king ascendant possible in order to ensure the perpetuation of the great works he has accomplished for the Northeastern Dragon Kingdom, even if that proves to be a champion other than one of his own offspring. A wise king will always choose the well-being of the many over the benefit of the one, and King J'Amal Aidin Kondur's wisdom is unassailable."

"In fewer than twenty hours, the Dragon Sleep will end, and the first challenge will begin in Ahl Sha H'Araah," said Jake, amazed that a month had passed so quickly. "If experience has taught me anything, that portion of the conference will take several hours before a victor emerges."

"You underestimate the difficulty of the challenge," stated T'Aer Bolun Dakkar. "We were only able to defeat the king's avatar in seven hours because of your obsession with developing new tactics and counter-tactics previously unseen in dragon history. Even King Tao Min Xiong's greatest avatar was unable to match the combination of your lightning fast analytical deductions combined with my aerial skills. We were victorious because your brilliance was never a part of any dragon's ancestral memories, and your insistence that we train so obsessively has enhanced my own power and agility a hundred-fold. King J'Amal Aidin Kondur has witnessed aspects of our battle techniques no other dragon could possibly have prepared for, and while that knowledge is largely incomplete, it is far beyond the comprehension of most, if not all of the contenders who have presented themselves for the conference. This will not be victory achieved in hours, Jake. It will continue for days, and it is highly possible that no dragon emerges from Ahl Sha H'Araah as a victor, but only the last to be defeated… which is still defeat," concluded T'Aer Bolun Dakkar."

"Which is why you've chosen to begin with that challenge," acknowledged Jake, enlightened. "It is truly the challenge that will separate the wheat from the chaff, and anyone who advances beyond it will do so with an elevated sense of respect and reverence for the Conference of Kings."

"Precisely," said T'Aer Bolun Dakkar. "Once the arrogance is stripped away from each challenger, they will themselves realize the serious and solemn nature of ruling a dragon kingdom, and from that moment, whoever emerges as the new dragon king ascendant will understand the burdens of a dragon king quite profoundly, and will rule accordingly," concluded T'Aer Bolun Dakkar.

For several hours, Jake and T'Aer Bolun Dakkar soared in the silence between Earth and the stars. Their minds, while eternally connected, simultaneously explored multiple layers of individual ponderance, chasing the edge of darkness that cloaked continent after continent on its ceaseless march around the globe.

As it approached the Himalaya Mountain Range, Jake and T'Aer Bolun Dakkar slowly descended into a natural arena known as The King's Courtyard, created by seven ice-bejeweled peaks at an altitude far above the prying eyes of all but the most adventurous of humans. Landing atop the highest of them, they drank in the indescribable beauty of The Crown of Earth.

"Such a fitting place to hold a Conference of Kings," said Jake.

They watched for several minutes as the mountainous arena began to fill with dragon kings and ambitious would-be dragon king ascendants. Shortly before midnight, King of Kings, T'Aer Bolun Dakkar flared his mighty wings, silently coming to rest in their midst before decloaking. Jake dismounted, sliding down the wing of his mighty dragon to join Svend Erickson and Sibyl Dupree at the edge of the arena.

Rearing onto his hind legs and flaring his massive wings out to his sides, King T'Aer Bolun Dakkar towered over the remaining dragons, boldly announcing, "This Conference of Kings for the Northeastern Dragon Kingdom, is now in session! Welcome, warriors all, and may the rightful king ascend!"

With T'Aer Bolun Dakkar's royal announcement, the infrequent sound of three dozen roaring dragons rose from the King's Courtyard into the night sky above The Crown of Earth.

CHAPTER 6

KING J'AMAL AIDIN KONDUR stood before the expectant eyes of over thirty dragons brimming with excitement at the prospect of ascending to his throne. Even with all three of his sons present and at the ready, he was admittedly impressed with the number and variety of additional warriors assembled inside the King's Courtyard.

"To all contenders assembled here, I bid you welcome," said King J'Amal Aidin Kondur. "While many have come, only one shall ascend and it is my wish and the hope of all dragons that the challenges presented will result in the selection of the best possible dragon king ascendant."

As he wandered through the field of ambitious prospects, the energy and excitement of the occasion were palpable. With each dragon clinging to every utterance of the regal dragon king, he began describing the first of the four challenges.

"The first challenge could also be the last for many if not most of you," said J'Amal Aidin Kondur. "Inside the transitional dimension of Ahl Sha H'Araah, you will each face my most deadly avatar, Danang. His skills are legendary, and he will show none of you even the smallest measure of mercy. Danang exists for the solitary purpose of destroying dragons. He will neither discriminate nor show favor to any of you. When you encounter him inside Ahl Sha H'Araah, do not hesitate for Danang most certainly will not."

After a long pause for the field of contenders to contemplate their strategies, King J'Amal Aidin Kondur continued, saying, "Beyond the veil of Ahl Sha H'Araah, you will each find an arena of your own. Danang will attack at the opportunity of his choosing, and the battle will continue until one or the other of you has been terminated. If you awaken to find yourself here in this courtyard, Danang will have been victorious and you will have failed. If only one of you succeeds in defeating Danang, all who did not, will be eliminated."

"There is no time limit for this challenge," said King J'Amal Aidin Kondur. "It will end when the final contender either awakens here or returns to the courtyard under their own power." With a final glance to survey the field of anxious warriors, he said, "Let the first challenge begin."

With varying degrees of enthusiasm, each dragon vanished into the realm of Ahl Sha H'Araah. The first of them reappeared only seconds after his departure, followed by a handful of others who awakened just as shocked and disoriented on the frozen floor of the courtyard. After that, they appeared in increasingly lengthy intervals. Minutes turned to hours, during which time a handful of the quickly dispatched dragons, realizing how unprepared and underequipped they had been, simply disappeared into the night.

The first of J'Amal Aidin Kondur's sons, J'Mir Mahajan, reappeared after nearly ten hours, closely followed by Na'Desh D'Monicus. An hour later, T'Aru Malka'Am and K'Zahn D'Monicus regained consciousness on the frozen ground, leaving only Mi'Kah D'Monicus, and T'Pal and Mi'Kael Mahajan unaccounted for inside Ahl Sha H'Araah.

King J'Amal Aidin Kondur released the dragons waiting patiently inside the courtyard so they could eat and rest to regain their strength. He would emit the tug of familiarity to recall them the moment the final warrior emerged, either in victory or defeat. Sixty hours into the challenge, Mi'Kah D'Monicus awakened beside Mi'Kael Mahajan, neither of whom were certain which of them had been deposited there first.

Inside Ahl Sha H'Araah, T'Pal Mahajan and Danang had been entangled in battle non-stop for nearly three full days. The ferocity with which they engaged one another was beyond anything T'Pal had ever imagined. Danang was fast, and his movements were fluid and graceful. He seemed impervious to fatigue and even after their seventy-hour slugfest, he showed no indication of tiring.

T'Pal spotted Danang's vulnerability only minutes into their battle but spotting it and reaching it were two entirely different matters. Danang had been bonded at some point and the bonding scale was missing. Although he had come close on multiple attempts, Danang protected that singular vulnerability with the determination of a psychopath. Every tactic T'Pal utilized was met by an equally effective parry from Danang. After days spent keeping Danang's attacks at bay, T'Pal realized the error he had been making repeatedly during the entire course of their battle. He had been keeping Danang at a distance when what he actually needed was to get closer to him. As he had done so often before, T'Pal was overthinking his actions and by avoiding Danang's proximity, he was preventing himself from reaching the only opening in the avatar's armor.

With his energy fading, T'Pal intentionally dropped his guard, allowing Danang to snatch him from mid-flight. Twisting in the powerful avatars grip, he managed to sink a single claw into the unprotected opening in Danang's chest. The avatar screamed out in pain before sinking his razor-sharp teeth into T'Pal's jugular and diving sharply downward.

T'Pal was bleeding out and considering the dizzying altitude from which they were descending, he realized he was unlikely to survive the impact against the jagged rocks lining the cliffs along the seashore beneath them. Nevertheless, T'Pal fought on, sinking his talon deeper and deeper into the weakening avatar's chest. He could feel the cool updraft of the air rising from the black water beneath them. With a final thrust, he felt his talon puncture the lining of the avatar's heart, just as his body was impaled onto the rocks at terminal velocity.

Moments later, he opened his eyes to find himself sprawled across the frozen floor of the King's Courtyard. Slowly rising from the ground, he noticed there were fewer than a dozen dragons observing him, and both of his brothers, J'Mir and Mi'Kael were beaming.

"Are we the only ones who have emerged so far?" puzzled T'Pal in abject disbelief. "How is that even possible?"

"The dragons you see here," said Mi'Kael, "are the only ones left who are willing to continue."

"You were the final challenger to emerge," said J'Mir. "Most of the others conceded and left days ago."

"How long have you two been waiting here?" asked T'Pal.

"Oh, I've only been here a few minutes," said Mi'Kael with a smile.

"Yes. Seven-hundred-twenty of them," responded J'Mir.

"Says he who lasted only ten hours!" countered Mi'Kael, jovially.

As the three dragon siblings joined the handful of remaining contenders at the center of the King's Courtyard, Kings J'Amal Aidin Kondur and T'Aer Bolun Dakkar descended from the seventh peak of The Crown of Earth, landing silently among them.

"Well done, champions!" said T'Aer Bolun Dakkar. "You have all battled bravely against the avatar of King J'Amal Aidin Kondur, and the fact that you are still here, is a testament to your tenacity. A wise king must understand that victory is not always possible; however, there is no dishonor in learning from defeat. You have all learned an important lesson in which patience was the true challenge. It is the most important quality of a dragon king who will inevitably rule for a thousand years. Without the patience to persevere through defeat, the joys of victory will always ring hollow, no matter how often they are celebrated."

"In the beginning, many gathered here were worried that another dragon would eliminate the remaining challengers with a victory," continued T'Aer Bolun Dakkar. "From the peaks above, I observed all of you as some disappeared into the night never to return while others, all of whom are still here, remained so as not to miss the emergence of the remaining contenders. After the first two days, those who initially feared a victor would eliminate them personally, began to evolve having experienced the fury of King J'Amal Aidin Kondur's avatar first-hand. You began to cheer them on. Even I could feel your disappointment when Mi'Kah D'Monicus and Mi'Kael Mahajan were defeated after sixty hours of intense combat and still, all of you remained.

"For twelve hours, you fevered with him," said T'Aer Bolun Dakkar. "Knowing the determination and energy required to continue against a foe all of you were certain was invincible, you remained with hope in your hearts, willing to concede victory to the dragon who would finally end Danang's destructive rampage. What you did not know; what you could not observe as I could inside the vastness of Ahl Sha H'Araah, is that T'Pal did, with his very last breath, destroy the avatar, Danang. He pierced its heart with a single talon, unwilling to surrender even as the avatar impaled him against the dagger-like rocks protruding from the shore. Although he was unable to complete the task of returning to the King's Courtyard under his own power, were Danang required to emerge and claim victory, he could not have."

In the faces of the remaining contenders, a visible change was evident. Gone were the false bravado and haughty demeanors of the privileged. They were all equals who had been bathed in the fire of defeat yet emerged from it stronger and more determined than ever before. Now, they were all dragons truly worthy of ascending to the northeastern throne, and in the Conference of Kings, J'Amal Aidin Kondur, Kai Bok Katari, Sha'Kaa Santiago, and T'Aer Bolun Dakkar could not have been more proud of them.

"The next challenge will begin in twenty-four hours," said T'Aer Bolun Dakkar. "Until then, eat, rest, and rejoice in knowing that among the brave warriors assembled here tonight, all are worthy. Although only one of you will ascend, each of you will know that he who does, will lead with the wisdom expected of a true dragon king."

Without another word, Jake, Sibyl, and Svend swung astride their dragons and disappeared into the Himalayan sky, followed by a collection of the finest dragons on Earth.

CHAPTER 7

JAKE AND T'AER BOLUN DAKKAR were also quite fatigued after several days of waiting atop the Crown of Earth. Their journey back to Nin'Jahlah culminated with a deep dive into the glassy waters of the Nin'Jahlan Sea where T'Aer Bolun Dakkar ate his fill of herring before exiting the water to take his place amid the tribe.

The hour was late, and the children were sleeping when Danni met Jake at the doorway of their simple but welcoming home. After kissing Jake, she said, "That was an awfully long conference. Were you able to determine who would be the new ascendant?"

With a tired smile, Jake replied, "That was only the first of four challenges. The conference will continue with the next challenge after the remaining dragons have eaten and rested for a full day."

Ushering Jake into the dining room where she had prepared a bountiful meal for him, Danni said, "The two of you must be exhausted. I had no idea the Conference of Kings would be so extensive."

"Nor did I," replied Jake. "I suppose I should have expected it though. Dragon ceremonies are steeped in traditions that are literally millions of years old. Choosing an ascendant dragon king would logically be one of the most significant events of a generation for them."

"True," said Danni. "I often forget that you met T'Aer Bolun Dakkar when you were eleven, and it was nearly ten years later when he ascended with you."

"Yes, and he was already a century old at the time," Jake replied. "By the time our real-world training began, he had already defeated well over a hundred challengers."

As she watched Jake partaking of the fish, fruits, and vegetables, grown in their own little Garden of Eden, she said, "It seems so out of character for him. I mean, I know his ascendance to dragon king was no cakewalk, but the reverence he holds for all life, and his absolute reluctance to harm anyone or anything makes it difficult to imagine him in a fight. Not that I believe he's a pushover or anything, but T'Aer Bolun Dakkar is such a gentle giant. His instinct is to save everyone, which makes it hard for me to imagine him in the heat of battle."

"T'Aer Bolun Dakkar, and King of Kings T'Aer Bolun Dakkar, are two vastly different sides of the same coin," said Jake. "For him, there is no such thing as 'the heat of battle' because I've never seen anyone, or anything succeed in engaging him for more than a few seconds. Other than when he was gassed by dragoneers, I've never even seen him vulnerable. Legend has it that when his father, Tao Min Xiong, banished King NaDahl D'Monicus to the Southern Ocean, NaDahl left with little objection because Tao Min Xiong would have singlehandedly slaughtered every dragon in the Northeastern Dragon Kingdom, had he resisted. T'Aer Bolun Dakkar possesses all the skill and cunning of Tao Min Xiong, plus a plethora of additional battle skills and experiences unseen by any other dragon king in history."

"You mean those things the two of you were working on when you would disappear for months at a time?" asked Danni with a knowing smile.

"Maybe," said Jake, winking at her. "But I'll never tell."

In the unparalleled tranquility of Nin'Jahlah, the Payne family, the tribe, and the King of Kings T'Aer Bolun Dakkar, all rested peacefully. A dimension away, a Hydra Dragoness named Xiana Safir was anything but peaceful. In fact, she was livid. After summoning all her sons, only Na'Desh appeared to inform her that he would be withdrawing from the conference.

"You will do no such thing!" screamed the Dragoness, barely able to contain her boiling rage. "The offspring of Xiana Safir do not surrender after only a single challenge!"

"I am not surrendering," explained Na'Desh. "I am withdrawing, for there are many others who would better serve as king of the Northeastern Dragon Kingdom. It is not an act of capitulation to acknowledge the nobility of others."

"You, Na'Desh, are the descendant of royalty! The blood of kings flows through your very veins! Nobility is your birthright!" railed the furious Hydra Dragoness, for once finding a subject all six of her heads could agree upon.

"Mother, for three days I stood in the presence of kings and warriors after battling an avatar of King J'Amal Aidin Kondur," explained Na'Desh. "After ten hours of relentless aerial, terrestrial, and aquatic combat, I assumed I would be one of the last to emerge, only to discover I was one of the first. There were challengers who lasted, not hours longer than I, but days! In the end, I cheered for them all. Not only for K'Zahn and Mi'Kah, but for all of them."

"And what of K'Zahn and Mi'Kah? Why did they ignore my summons?" demanded Xiana Safir.

"They are still contenders and forbidden to congregate outside the King's Courtyard," Na'Desh explained. "In answering your summons, they would have disqualified and dishonored themselves."

"I am their mother!" screamed Xiana Safir from one of her many impatient mouths.

"J'Amal Aidin Kondur is their king!" retorted Na'Desh. "He is the king they hope one day to become, and you are only making things more difficult for them. While other contenders are resting for the next challenge, K'Zahn and Mi'Kah are unable to recover because you selfishly continue to demand of them, that which they cannot give you: Their presence."

"So, I must placate myself with the most pathetic of my offspring," hissed Xiana Safir dismissively.

"No, Mother," replied Na'Desh. "You must placate yourself with the over-abundance of your own heads containing an inadequate supply of wisdom, for I assure you; you will never see me again. Goodbye, Mother."

Na'Desh D'Monicus vanished into the night sky without so much as a final glance in Xiana Safir's direction. After spending three days surrounded by valiant and honorable dragons, he could no longer ignore the poisonous vitriol he had endured for nearly a century under the scrutiny of her six condescending heads. Somehow, the short flight to his roost in Nepal seemed more liberating than it ever had before. It was as if he could finally see the stars formerly invisible to him, due to his gaze pointing ever downward in subjugation to an overbearing mother. Within minutes of landing in Nepal, Na'Desh was sound asleep.

After a long recuperative slumber, ten aspiring dragon king ascendants presented inside the King's Courtyard tucked away among the snowy peaks of the Himalayas. With the other regional dragon kings already assembled, Jake and T'Aer Bolun Dakkar descended into the arena, taking their place among them.

"Welcome noble warriors all!" exclaimed King T'Aer Bolun Dakkar. "I trust you are well-rested and ready to proceed with the flag challenge. King Sha'Kaa Santiago will explain the contest, and on behalf of us all, may the rightful dragon ascend."

As King T'Aer Bolun Dakkar ceded centerstage, King Sha'Kaa Santiago stepped forward to address the expectant contenders.

"Today, you will each choose an avatar to represent you beyond the veil of dragons where you might inadvertently encounter humans," said King Sha'Kaa Santiago. "While it is wise to choose an avatar indigenous to the northeastern realm, it will not be the avatar from which you draw your strength, but rather the heart of the dragon inside it. Since you are all quite familiar with the animals common to your region, there are obviously a number of excellent choices to consider."

King Sha'Kaa Santiago allowed them a few minutes to visualize an avatar they felt would be familiar to their region while projecting the degree of distinction and prowess worthy of a dragon king. A few of them had made their decisions long ago, but others had refrained, hoping to glean a deeper understanding of the purpose their avatars would serve. In fact, there were even those who had yet to make their choices, electing to decide on the ground when they reached the challenge theater.

"This challenge will be terrestrial and the use of your wings in any manner will result in your immediate disqualification," explained King Sha'Kaa Santiago. "As with the battle evaluation, only those who can secure a flag before my bonded rider and I can acquire one, will move on to the next challenge. Should we; however, manage to reach the flag location first, we will take them all and each of you will have failed this portion of the challenge. Of course, if everyone fails, no one will be eliminated, but neither will any of you be considered victorious."

It was obvious that each contender was determined to reach the coordinates and secure a flag of their own before Sibyl and King Sha'Kaa Santiago arrived and terminated the challenge. While they were somewhat intimidated by King Sha'Kaa Santiago himself, they were certain his bonded rider would be unable to maintain the pace of a dragon king, and therefore, victory seemed well within reach for them.

Each dragon was given start coordinates at points located equidistantly from the predetermined spot where the ten flags were planted. The spot was more than familiar to Sibyl and Sha'Kaa Santiago. In fact, it was a secluded meadow exactly five miles from Sibyl's farmhouse, and thirty miles from the various starting points for the assembly of dragons. For the past month, Sibyl and Sha'Kaa had meticulously surveyed the challenge area to identify starting points that ensured equal levels of difficulty for each contender. Together, they had personally negotiated each route several times at full speed, to make sure their calculations were indeed equitable for each challenger. Even after allowing for unforeseen obstacles and distractions, there was neither an advantage nor a disadvantage to be gained from being assigned any particular course.

After informing the contenders of their individual starting locations, King Sha'Kaa Santiago explained, "Once everyone has reached their assigned coordinates, King T'Aer Bolun Dakkar will emit a tug of familiarity signaling for the race to begin. You will need to use the maps in your genetic memory to find your way to him, and I'd suggest you move swiftly, because it would be unwise to underestimate the speed at which Sibyl and I will cover that same distance. Above all, remember this. You are dragons. The longer you remain in the form of your avatar, the easier it becomes to accept its limitations as your own. Do not succumb to that temptation, or you will lose! This I promise you!"

CHAPTER 8

MOMENTS AFTER KING SHA'KAA SANTIAGO'S challenge explanation, Jake, Svend, and Sibyl mounted their respective dragon kings and vanished into the thinly oxygenated skies above the Himalayas. As they flew south from the arid elevations of Northern Asia into the dense humidity of South America, it was the first time many of the young dragons had ever been outside the regions of their birth. Dragons accustomed to breathing in the thin upper atmosphere of the Himalayan Mountain Range, were already feeling sluggish and unexpectedly fatigued in the tropical and isothermal climate of the Columbian Rainforest when they reached their designated start coordinates.

After morphing into their selected avatars, Mi'Kael Mahajan had chosen the Asiatic cheetah and T'Pal Mahajan, like his father, assumed the form of a Bengal tiger. Surprisingly, J'Mir Mahajan had chosen the Przewalski's horse, a rare and endangered species long thought to have been extinct in the wild.

The two remaining sons of Xiana Safir, K'Zahn and Mi'Kah D'Monicus, had selected the Arctic Fox and the Snow Leopard, respectively, and T'Aru Malka'Am, a descendant of the great warrior, Se'Thaa Malka'Am, morphed into the form of an Arctic ferret. Two dragon contenders from the distant Gobi Desert in Mongolia, Ra'Haku Manchu, and Bao Batbayar, both selected Black Tailed Gazelles as their avatars although they were mutually unaware that they had chosen the same animal. Rounding off the group of ten dragons were A'Tal Batang as a Siberian Tiger, and Bo'Ka Madura in the avatar of a Komodo Dragon.

Having been unable to view the avatars of one another, each contender was unaware of the forms their adversaries had taken. Furthermore, none of them had even the faintest idea as to which of those avatars was that of King Sha'Kaa Santiago, making it impossible to know who they had to beat to the flag location. Judging by the stifling atmospheric conditions they would all need to overcome; it was clear why King Sha'Kaa Santiago had advised them to move quickly. Regardless of their chosen avatars, the Southwestern Dragon King and his bonded rider would clearly have an advantage over the remaining field of challengers. Not only were they absolutely familiar with the terrain ahead of them, but they were also accustomed to the regional climate and would most assuredly use that knowledge and experience to their benefit.

Shortly after assuming their animal alter-egos, each of the challengers felt the unmistakable tug of familiarity issued by T'Aer Bolun Dakkar in a massive pulse that extended outward from him for nearly fifty miles in each direction. The intense wave created a genetic beacon that was irresistible, revealing his exact location and the distance they must travel to reach him.

All the avatars rushed into the dense vegetation of the Columbian Rainforest, following the genetically inherited global positioning system that would lead them unerringly to their final destinations. After only a few minutes, many of the avatars were overwhelmed at the extreme difference between the climactic conditions of their customary regions as compared to the heavily oxygenated, humid environment in which they currently found themselves. Most of the predatory feline avatars quickly discovered their limitations. While exceptionally well suited to stunning bursts of speed, they could only maintain that velocity for short distances before exhausting themselves. With thirty miles to cover, they were forced to limit the amount of energy expended so as not to deplete their avatars before they could complete the race.

The gazelles were faring particularly well until midway through the race when they realized, even in South America, gazelles were prey inside a rainforest teeming with hungry nocturnal predators. Neither of them would even reach the glade before being seized upon; one by wolves and the other by a jaguar seemingly lying in wait for him. In order to free themselves, they were forced to abandon their avatars and reveal their true forms, which led to their immediate disqualification.

Through a stroke of pure genius, T'Aru Malka'Am was the first to reach the meadow and secure one of the coveted flags. His Arctic ferret avatar was so obviously out of place on the floor of the rainforest, it had been snatched from the ground by an enormous horned owl! In what could most accurately have been described as a veiled threat, T'Aru Malka'Am convinced the owl that carrying him to the clearing would be much better for him than being eaten in mid-air by a dragon. Sure enough, the Arctic ferret was the first to reach the destination and claim his flag.

Although the Przewalski's horse avatar chosen by J'Mir Mahajan was by no means as explosive as the Bengal tiger or as cunning as the Arctic fox running neck and neck with him, the horse's consistent gallop had effectively chewed up the distance while maintaining a constant tempo, unsustainable by the majority of the other animals attempting to claim a coveted flag. As they approached the clearing only steps ahead of Sibyl Dupree and the Black Wolf, the final hundred meters became an all-out dash. The three contenders suddenly remembered they were still dragons despite the physical limitations of the avatars they had chosen. In a four-way tie, they all reached their destination, surprised to find a teacup chihuahua and an Arctic ferret already waiting there at the center of the clearing when they collected their flags.

Shortly after King Sha'Kaa Santiago secured the remaining flags, the last of the eligible contenders emerged from the tangled wall of trees at the edge of the clearing, albeit too late. Having disqualified themselves, both gazelles respectfully waited until all the others had completed the challenge before exiting the forest and joining them.

With twelve eclectic animals gathered in the secluded glade, each of them was curious as to the identities of the winners. The first to reveal himself was the black wolf, King Sha'Kaa Santiago, having already exposed his identity when he removed the remaining flags and ended the challenge. Next, to the shock and amazement of the remaining contenders, the tiny chihuahua unfolded, revealing the domineering presence of King T'Aer Bolun Dakkar.

Shortly thereafter, Kings J'Amal Aidin Kondur and Kai Bok Katari descended into the clearing, having monitored the actions of each avatar during the challenge from overhead.

Once everyone was assembled in the glade, King T'Aer Bolun Dakkar said, "Although only four of you have qualified for the next challenge, it has been an honor to bear witness to each of your performances and the comportment with which you have all conducted yourselves."

After a brief pause, he continued, saying, "The first to claim a flag was the Arctic ferret, T'Aru Malka'Am!" exclaimed T'Aer Bolun Dakkar as the young challenger unfolded from his animal avatar.

"Next, was the Przewalski's horse avatar of J'Mir Mahajan," stated T'Aer Bolun Dakkar as J'Mir revealed himself.

"The final two challengers to secure a flag were the Arctic fox, K'Zahn D'Monicus and the Bengal tiger, T'Pal Mahajan!" exclaimed King T'Aer Bolun Dakkar as they unfolded to stand with T'Aru and J'Mir.

"To all who are present," said T'Aer Bolun Dakkar, "these honorable contenders have successfully completed the second challenge and will advance to the third round. Let it be known, that one who now stands before you, shall ascend to the throne of the Northeastern Dragon King, for all of them are worthy."

One by one, the remaining dragons unfolded from the forms of their avatars to congratulate the champions of the day. Before departing the lush green wilderness visible for dragons despite the darkness cloaking the Columbian countryside, T'Aer Bolun Dakkar announced, "The challenges will resume two nights from now in the King's Courtyard. Until then, brave warriors, eat, rest, and be well."

Seconds later, the clearing was void of all but two occupants.

"Your endurance has improved dramatically over the past few years, Sibyl," said King Sha'Kaa Santiago.

"I've been blessed with an excellent mentor," Sibyl replied. "Even though you did give them a five-minute head start," she added, winking at Sha'Kaa who had already reverted to his avatar.

"And what about that trick with the owl?" asked Sibyl as the two of them dashed into the thick jungle.

"Ingenious!" exclaimed Sha'Kaa; their footsteps trailing off into the distance as they skillfully navigated the familiar terrain on their way back to the farmhouse.

"And then there were four," said Jake as he and T'Aer Bolun Dakkar passed through the inter-dimensional rift into Ahl Sha H'Araah. A moment later, they reappeared alongside Kings J'Amal Aidin Kondur and Kai Bok Katari outside the lair of Bokur D'Monicus.

The sinking feeling of having one dragon king parked outside your lair, pales in comparison to having three of them there. When Bokur D'Monicus hesitantly appeared to face the council of dragon royalty who had called him to the carpet, his sheepish demeanor instantly revealed the consciousness of his own guilt.

It was King J'Amal Aidin Kondur who spoke first, saying, "Bokur D'Monicus, twice you have inserted yourself into matters pertaining to the Conference of Kings. It would be unwise of you to make a third attempt."

To his credit, Bokur D'Monicus remained silent during the dressing down he was receiving from King J'Amal Aidin Kondur. Obviously, the propaganda he had spread at the behest of Xiana Safir during the first challenge had not escaped the watchful eyes of the three unexpected visitors.

T'Aer Bolun Dakkar spoke next, saying, "Your son, K'Zahn D'Monicus, requires neither your assistance nor your interference as a contender, but the avatars you inserted in the flag challenge have derailed the opportunities of challengers much more honorable than you. The only wolf within the farmland of Sibyl Dupree is the Avatar of King Sha'Kaa Santiago, and no Jaguar would dare risk the wrath of an angry dragon king by trespassing on the property of his bonded rider. The dragons you dispatched to eliminate Ra'Haku Manchu and Bao Batbayar from the competition by attacking their gazelle avatars, were sloppy and heavy-handed. King Kai Bok Katari spotted your agents as they entered the challenge arena, and abstained from destroying them, only because they were being manipulated by you and your Hydra Dragoness mate."

"K'Zahn is a dedicated warrior and he would make a fine dragon king ascendant," said King J'Amal Aidin Kondur. "However, your interference jeopardizes not only *his* standing, but that of the entire D'Monicus bloodline. So far, your actions have not even influenced K'Zahn's challenge results, which makes the reasoning behind them even more confusing. Nevertheless, should you or your surrogates continue your surreptitious campaign of meddling, I will take action to ensure both you and Xiana Safir are held accountable."

For the three dragon kings, there was no expectation of a response from Bokur D'Monicus. Accordingly, King J'Amal Aidin Kondur departed with King Kai Bok Katari and Svend. T'Aer Bolun Dakkar and Jake lingered with Bokur D'Monicus until the others had vanished into the night.

"I met your father," said King T'Aer Bolun Dakkar.

Bokur D'Monicus looked as if he had seen a ghost. With a trembling voice, he asked, "How... How do you know my father?"

"There is a highly confidential matter that he entrusted to me before requesting that I seal him inside is burial chamber," said King T'Aer Bolun Dakkar. "Despite his lapse in judgement over five centuries ago, NaDahl D'Monicus evolved beyond his transgressions and justifiably reclaimed the mantle of a wise and beloved king. I can personally attest to the fact that he was revered on a level any dragon king would find inspiring, and were he able to witness the comportment, honor, and dedication with which Na'Desh, Mi'Kah and K'Zahn conducted themselves during this Conference of Kings, he would have been exceedingly proud of them.

As King T'Aer Bolun Dakkar and Jake prepared to leave, the King of Kings said, "Bokur D'Monicus, your son, K'Zahn, does not need your interference. He needs your respect and encouragement, because whether he is selected as dragon king ascendant or not, you are his father... and he needs to know you care."

Long after Jake and King T'Aer Bolun Dakkar silently disappeared into the darkness overhead, Bokur D'Monicus remained outside his lair, staring blankly across the hundreds of peaks and valleys that make up the Himalayan Mountain Range. Centuries ago, King Tao Min Xiong had taken away the honor of the D'Monicus family bloodline. Tonight, his son, T'Aer Bolun Dakkar, had given it back to them.

CHAPTER 9

BOKUR D'MONICUS SPENT AN ENTIRE DAY allowing the weight of King T'Aer Bolun Dakkar's words to sink in. During that time, he remained in absolute isolation, ignoring even the insistent requests of Xiana Safir to meet with him. The realization that his own father had chosen another dragon to receive his confidential edict was an eye-opening revelation. Twice, NaDahl D'Monicus had summoned Bokur, and twice he had ignored that summons. The shame he felt at the mere mention of his father's name had replaced any remaining sense of paternal loyalty he may have harbored for him. Now, a dragon completely removed from the D'Monicus bloodline; the son of the very dragon king who had stripped him of his honor and banished him, was the one in which NaDahl D'Monicus had chosen to confide.

How short-sighted must he have been to believe a banished king would not have spent centuries reflecting on his failures? Unlike Bokur, NaDahl D'Monicus had accepted responsibility for the damage he had done to his own reputation and the reputations of his descendants. Conversely, Bokur was currently involved in the shaming of his children motivated purely by his own thirst for revenge, and the ambitions of a Hydra dragoness clearly rooted in vanity.

For well over one hundred years, he had been emotionally invested in sullying the reputations of Tao Min Xiong and his sole offspring, T'Aer Bolun Dakkar. In fact, he had been counted in the dozens of challengers quickly dispatched by the dragon king ascendant. Despite his embarrassingly brief battle with the younger, smaller dragon, T'Aer Bolun Dakkar never gloated over his victory or attempted to shame Bokur D'Monicus in any way. After their encounter, the dragon king ascendant deposited him in an uninhabited region of Iceland's barren interior, sparing him the humiliation of awakening under the scrutiny of his peers.

Rather than accepting the reality of his defeat, he, himself, began circulating rumors that T'Aer Bolun Dakkar had refused to accept his challenge. Even those boldly false assertions did not elicit a response, and before he appeared at Bokur D'Monicus's lair with the other two dragon kings, it had been nearly a half-century since they'd met face-to-face.

Suddenly, Bokur D'Monicus felt small. He felt lacking in the wisdom that had obviously skipped a generation, because his offspring were willing to re-earn the honor and nobility required of a king, whereas he felt it was simply due him. The daunting reality of T'Aer Bolun Dakkar's towering presence had removed all vestiges of doubt that he could even walk the footsteps of the king of dragon kings. Yet, possessing all the tools necessary to dismantle Bokur D'Monicus's carefully constructed web of duplicity, King T'Aer Bolun Dakkar instead revealed to him the very knowledge he needed to restore honor to the D'Monicus bloodline.

Later that evening, as K'Zahn D'Monicus exited the Indian Ocean after feeding, he was somewhat surprised to find his father in the sky above him when he emerged from the frigid waters. Silently, he accompanied the senior D'Monicus to the deserted King's Courtyard inside the Crown of Earth, lighting quietly beside him in the snow-covered basin.

After slowly rotating to take in the full range of the majestic beauty surrounding them, Bokur D'Monicus began to speak, saying, "For centuries, I have sought the solitude of this sanctuary in the clouds. Fifteen thousand years ago, our forefathers began convening The Tournament of Dragons here once every quarter century. It was a festive gathering of young male warriors competing for the favor of female dragons of mating age. Challengers from all four dragon kingdoms would converge on this location in numbers so vast, their wings would literally block out the sun. At the conclusion of the lunar cycle, the finalists would compete against the king's eldest son in a carefully choreographed theatrical bout, primarily for the ceremonial entertainment of all who were present. It was our way of strengthening the alliances of the dragon kingdoms as human civilizations began to expand across the globe.

Twelve-hundred years ago, the king's eldest son had been particularly interested in a beautiful dragoness who managed to thwart the advances of all prior suitors. In the final ceremonial event, the king's son was desperate to win her attention, and quickly escalated the mock battle into one lacking even the pretense of theatrics. His attacks became so vicious and lethal, the other dragon was forced to abandon the pre-scripted battle ballet, in order to defend himself. From there, things quickly spiraled out of control until both dragons were locked in a duel to the death; a duel in which an adolescent Tao Min Xiong ultimately killed the king's eldest son, T'Arus D'Monicus.

That was the last time the Tournament of Dragons was convened, and with the waning solidarity of the various kingdoms, humans felt empowered and encouraged to seek out and destroy dragons by the tens of thousands. To justify their actions, they blamed any and all manner of misfortunes on the dragon scourge, even as they killed each other in numbers far greater than the entire population of dragons ever had.

With denial serving as his only justification, T'Arus's younger sibling, NaDahl D'Monicus, attempted to overthrow King Tao Min Xiong and wrest control of his kingdom away from him. Having severely underestimated the Northwestern Dragon King, just as T'Arus had done, he was defeated, removed from power, and banished, never again to set foot in the Northeastern Dragon Kingdom."

After a long pause to absorb his father's comments, K'Zahn asked, "Why do you reveal such things to me on the eve of the next challenge in the Conference of Kings?"

"Because I do not wish for you to bear the false burden foisted onto the D'Monicus bloodline by T'Arus and perpetuated by NaDahl D'Monicus, as I have done," replied Bokur D'Monicus. "I have spent so many decades forcing you to become what I could not, because I was unwise and unworthy. You, my son, have displayed wisdom and discernment despite the walls of confusion erected by your mother and me. Our selfish agendas are an unfair and unjustified responsibility to place on the shoulders of you and your brothers. For years, I have known the truth, yet continued to peddle a false narrative in hopes of reclaiming something I have obviously never truly had: Honor."

Turning to face is son, Bokur D'Monicus said, "I am proud of you, K'Zahn. Proud that you are my spawn, and proud that you were able to set aside a false narrative and cling to what you know in your heart to be true. A dragon king is not born into royalty. He ascends to it by overcoming the snares, pitfalls, and obstacles, that test both his wisdom and his ability to rule. You have risen to the challenge, and whether or not you should ascend to the throne of King J'Amal Aidin Kondur, I am exceedingly proud of you, and honored to call you, Na'Desh, and Mi'Kah, my sons."

"Thank you, Father," said K'Zahn. "In my heart, I know you have only done what you felt was necessary to shield us from the scandals of our ancestors. It is natural for any father to shape the world in a manner that ensures the success of his children. Na'Desh, Mi'Kah and I are no longer whelps, and you have equipped us all with the knowledge and skills necessary to shape our own destinies. Now, we must navigate the paths we have chosen for ourselves. We ask only that you respect our choices and ultimately share in the joy of our accomplishments," K'Zahn concluded.

"Nothing less should be expected of any Father," replied Bokur D'Monicus. "And nothing less shall my sons receive from me."

The two dragons remained in the deserted arena for another hour, drinking in the idyllic beauty and serenity of their surroundings before finally ascending into the mist covered peaks of the frozen Himalayas. Burdens had been lifted from each of their shoulders, and their unencumbered journeys home had rarely been more peaceful.

With another full night before the resumption of the conference, both Jake and T'Aer Bolun Dakkar enjoyed their time relaxing and occupying themselves with the delightful distractions of Nin'Jahlah. From the front porch, Jake watched as the twins frolicked in the pasture that was their front yard, chasing the most coveted of their playthings... Turbo!

As the tiny chihuahua sprinted back and forth, he would allow Sammy and Jewel to get within inches of him, before quickly darting off in another direction as they chased after him, giggling hysterically. Tagging along behind the twins were a hundred hybrid dinosaurs jockeying for pole position while attempting to follow the erratic trail blazed by the children they so deeply adored.

Danni stood silently behind Jake, watching as he created magic with a bamboo cup packed with an assortment of polychromatic pencils. As mesmerizing as the images, themselves were, the process by which he created them was literally dizzying to observe. The speed and accuracy of his drawing technique allowed him to quickly capture moments in time that would otherwise have been but a fleeting image, lost to history in the blink of an eye. It was like watching an ambidextrous person write cursive with both hands simultaneously, but rather than capturing words, Jake captured paralyzingly vivid photorealistic images in the time it took the average person to write a note.

Their home was filled with such images, but to Danni, they never seemed to grow old. During the time they had been together, he had drawn the entire world for her, transporting her to places fewer than a half-percent of the world's population had ever seen. It was her constant reminder that there were still beautiful things in the world, even when challenging times threatened to overshadow them.

In a few short minutes, he'd created another artistic masterpiece that captured a place only four pairs of human eyes had ever seen, while their children frolicked in a field of dinosaurs pursuing the avatar of the most powerful dragon king to have ever walked the earth.

Tomorrow night, that same dragon would preside over the third challenge in the Conference of Kings, ensuring fairness and objectivity in the performance of his duties as the king of all dragon kings. Today, however, he was simply Turbo, romping in a magical pasture with the children he affectionately called The Prince of Ahl Sha H'Araah, and the Jewel of Nin'Jahlah.

CHAPTER 10

JUST AS THEY HAD DONE with the previous challenges, each contender arrived early, enthusiastically welcoming the next task. After the four dragon kings descended into the King's Courtyard, King Kai Bok Katari stepped forward to explain the challenge of the day.

"It is known as the Ivory Challenge," said the Southeastern Dragon King. "The entire journey will transpire inside the realm of Ahl Sha H'Araah, yet you will struggle to discern the difference between the challenge arena and the continents of Africa and Australia. As you will all remember quite vividly, the punishment inflicted by the king's avatar, Danang, was far from an illusion as it unfolded during the challenge. This arena will be no less convincing, and the decisions you make therein will be of no lesser impact than those made outside the realm of Ahl Sha H'Araah."

After giving the final four prospective dragon king ascendants time to reflect on their past experiences, King Kai Bok Katari continued, saying, "The challenge is actually quite simple in its description. Each of you will arrive at my roost near Adelaide, Australia upon passing through the interdimensional rift. From there, you will travel to Africa, where you will locate two ivory tusks and return with them to my roost. When your mission is complete, you will exit Ahl Sha H'Araah and return here, to the King's Courtyard."

To the four dragons receiving the instructions, the task seemed far too simple. There were several options on the table. The illegal ivory trade in Africa, although on the decline, was still relatively easy to access. There were also multiple depots where illegal ivory was stored after having been seized by the authorities during raids. Although none of the contenders voiced these concerns, the perplexed expressions on their faces spoke volumes regarding their consternation.

Interrupting their silent contemplation, King Kai Bok Katari said, "The challenge begins now, and may your journeys be successful."

One after another, the four dragons vanished into the interdimensional rift of Ahl Sha H'Araah, instantly appearing in the skies above Kai Bok Katari's roost. After circling briefly, the dragons embarked upon their journey across the Indian Ocean, passing over Madagascar and into the southern region of Africa.

K'Zahn D'Monicus was immediately struck by the near primal beauty of the massive continent. The variety of wildlife visible from his vantage point two thousand meters above the savanna was stunning, actually distracting him from his clearly defined mission. There were giraffes and zebras, gazelles and antelopes, prides of lions and an incalculable number of different species of birds. They all seemed to move in concert with one another, performing some predefined and beautifully executed dance conducted by an unseen producer. The thick aroma of sun-drenched grasses combined with the earthy smells of the animals grazing upon them, drifted upward, assailing the senses of the hovering dragon as the rising thermals kept him aloft.

The appearance of an elephant herd approaching in the distance captured K'Zahn's attention, reminding him of the mission he had been dispatched to complete. The giant mammals were regal in their appearance, moving slowly to avoid outpacing the two young calves in their midst. Scanning the horizon briefly, he caught a glint of sunlight reflecting from something at the crest of the hillside overlooking the well-worn path travelled by the elephants. Looking closer, he recognized two men wearing gilly suits lying in a prone position, hiding in the grass.

Horror gripped K'Zahn but quickly morphed into anger as he realized the men were hunters, hoping to take down the bull at the front of the herd for his ivory tusks! They were going to kill him right in front of his babies!

Cloaking, K'Zahn quickly descended, hoping to intervene and somehow prevent the tragedy unfolding before him; however, the muzzle flash in the distance indicated the deadly round had been sent. Both K'Zahn and the projectile were headed in the same direction, but with different objectives in mind. The adrenalin rushing through his veins pushed him to a previously unattained velocity, allowing him to intercept the deadly round by swooping in front of the bull elephant at the very last possible fraction of a second.

The large caliber round impacted K'Zahn's dragon hide, flattening and falling inertly to the ground as the men on the hilltop chambered and sent another round. K'Zahn swatted the second bullet to the ground as he headed directly toward the cowardly sniper hiding nearly a mile away from his target. The precision with which he snatched the rifle from the shooter's grip left both him and his spotter frightened and bewildered. Seconds later, the remnants of the rifle came raining down from the sky above them in several barely recognizable pieces.

Abandoning their illegal poaching expedition, both men broke cover, frantically rushing down the back side of the hill to the location where they had parked their vehicle. It was exactly where they'd left it; however, the two-ton boulder now occupying the back seat looked as if it had been dropped from a hundred feet overhead, snapping both the rear axle and the driveshaft when it impacted. Graciously, K'Zahn had left their radio in working condition, but they were miles from civilization, so they would be spending this night at the bottom of the food chain rather than at the top of it.

In the distance, the small herd of elephants made their way through the kill zone and down into the safety of a ravine sheltered by Umbrella Thorn Acacia trees. Not that they had reason to worry about the hunters anymore. Those two gentlemen would be cowering inside their immobilized vehicle until help arrived the next morning. With any luck, they would strongly reconsider embarking on another such frivolous adventure anytime soon, if ever.

T'Aru Malka'Am was just as awestruck when Madagascar and the African coast loomed large in front of him after crossing the vast emptiness of the Indian Ocean. He had completely forgotten this was a simulated reality the moment he appeared over Adelaide, and despite his attempt to keep that fact in focus, he was unable to. The very real scenery parading before his golden eyes was more spectacular than anything he had ever seen, and its unspoiled beauty instantly gripped him.

The abundant wildlife populating the savanna below moved to the pace of an unwritten and unheard orchestra with nature dictating the tempo. He was observing a massive herd of water buffalo moving in unison toward their favorite watering hole when suddenly, they all stopped. Looking ahead of the herd, he spotted her in the distance. Even from his perspective high above the terrain bathed in the golden light of a slowly setting sun, he could see the distress in the female elephant's eyes.

She was agitatedly pacing up and down the edge of a muddy bank that had apparently given away without warning. Flying closer, he spotted her calf. The clumsy baby elephant had been curiously peering over the edge at the water below when the bank collapsed, having been partially eroded from recent rains. The calf was frantically attempting to drag himself from the mud as his terrified voice called out to his mother in despair. Each time she approached the unstable edge, more of the bank gave way beneath her, dumping even more debris onto her terrified baby. Her attention was divided between keeping the other animals from approaching and scanning the bank for a way to reach the calf, slowly being sucked deeper and deeper into the unforgiving mud.

In a final act of desperation, the mother elephant ran towards the bank, intending to jump over the edge and rescue her sinking child. Unable to sustain the weight of the charging elephant, the ground gave way beneath her and she tumbled over the edge. The horror of her miscalculation dawned on her as she fell, headed straight for her struggling calf below. Her rescue attempt was about to kill him.

T'Aru Malka'Am caught her in mid-fall, carrying the astonished elephant up and away from the muddy gulch attempting to swallow her calf. Setting her down onto more stable ground, the dragon quickly returned, carefully latching onto, and lifting the struggling calf from the deadly trap. Seconds later the calf and his mother were reunited as she wrapped her trunk around him, pulling him beneath her to safety.

T'Aru Malka'Am landed a few meters away from them in the tall golden hued grass. Once the mother elephant was satisfied that her calf was uninjured, she looked up, making direct eye contact with the dragon who had curiously appeared out of nowhere to rescue her and her baby. As their gazes locked, the enormous precipice between the languages of a dragon and an elephant meant nothing, because gratitude is not defined by words.

With a final glance, T'Aru Malka'Am took to the sky and the mother elephant led her calf down a gentle slope to the water's edge where, together, they drank.

J'Mir Mahajan was gripped by the same sense of astonishment upon entering the southern African theater. The multitude of colors and sights and sounds and smells, were like inhaling the combined history of the world with each breath taken. It felt to him as if simply being in Africa had already begun to change him. As the group's compulsive diplomat, J'Mir spent nearly the entire journey crossing the Indian Ocean in deep contemplation, searching for a way to fulfill the terms of the challenge without harming the creatures endowed with those magnificent ivory masterpieces.

So enthralled was J'Mir by the variations in the continental topography, he was already crossing over the rainforest of Congo when he spotted the elderly bull elephant. The magnificent creature had obviously lived a full life and was nearing his final days when J'Mir spotted him separating himself from the herd. Just as dragons have done for millions of years, he began the unspoken voyage of the dying, wandering off into the dense foliage of the forest he had called home for nearly seven decades. While the rest of the herd *did* notice his departure, they did not follow; thereby allowing their final memories of him to serve as a tribute to his long and distinguished life.

The tired elephant walked for hours, covering miles and miles of ground beneath the lush green canopy of trees overhead. The few animals encountered by the regal pachyderm, respectfully ceded a path for him, comprehending the significance of the elephant's final journey.

J'Mir was so enraptured by the African giant, he found it impossible to abandon the creature before it had reached its final destination. The elephant slowed as it approached an area beneath a stand of great moabi trees reaching nearly sixty meters into the sky above. There in the rich, soft soil beneath a ceiling of lush green leaves, the once mighty elephant stopped and laid down. Overhead, the branches seemed as if they had interlocked to afford the passing guardian a degree of privacy as their leaves rustled peacefully in the gentle summer breeze.

The sound of an approaching helicopter shattered the near perfect serenity of the moment as it neared the location of the exhausted soul below. Although the elephant had clearly heard the aircraft approaching, the long journey had left him completely exhausted, lacking even the strength to stand. While the pilot searched for a location in which to land, J'Mir slipped between the branches overhead, lighting only a few feet from the reposed elephant. As their eyes met, the dying elephant's expression revealed his final thoughts, wishing only to pass in peace before the greedy ivory pirates began hacking off his tusks.

J'Mir came closer, lying down beside him. Expanding his wings, he gently embraced the dying creature. "Sleep, my friend," said J'Mir, unsure whether the passing beast could understand him. As the helicopter landed in a nearby clearing and the crew of ivory thieves poured out of it, J'Mir cloaked, and he and the elephant vanished.

The small group of men seemed perplexed at the absence of the elephant they had been tracking. The radio transmitter they tagged him with days earlier, had led them to this location before the signal unexpectedly disappeared. They surveyed the clearing and the surrounding area for nearly an hour, often coming within feet of J'Mir and his protected charge. Finding nothing, the men's frustration was evident in their heated discussion as they cursed the antiquated technology on the way back to their helicopter. J'Mir remained with the elephant long after it had expired. When he unwrapped his wings, it appeared to be resting peacefully, having passed in its sleep.

    J'Mir located the radio transmitter and destroyed it before digging a spacious grave for the noble beast using his bare claws. The grave was so deep, it would likely be discovered after a million years by archeologists who would wonder how it had even gotten there.

CHAPTER 11

K'ZAHN D'MONICUS, T'ARU MALKA'AM, AND J'MIR MAHAJAN were all headed back to King Kai Bok Katari's roost near Adelaide. In the meantime, T'Pal was deep in thought, carefully contemplating his next actions. Unlike his competitors, he had seen nothing of the beauty observed by his rivals. The thick black smoke rising from the interior of Tanzania, greeted him even before he reached the eastern coast of the African continent. A lightning strike had set an area of dried grass ablaze between Lake Victoria and the western edge of the Serengeti National Park. With the abundance of dried grass to fuel the fire, it spread quickly, igniting hundreds of acres into a rapidly advancing wall of flame. Once his eyes could finally pierce the veil of grey, the number of panicked animals attempting to escape the savage fire ripping across the landscape was terrifying to observe, even for a dragon.

T'Pal quickly launched into action, working to slow the flames that forced faster animals to flee eastward, and trapping slower ones inside a rapidly tightening noose of unforgiving fire. Flying into the wall of flames sweeping across the plentiful tinder provided by the grassy expanse of the Serengeti, T'Pal ingested as much of the ash and charred residue left behind as possible. Using it to fuel his own fiery regurgitations, he ignited counter fires, burning a wide path into the landscape to deplete the area of fuel for the steadily advancing inferno.

After setting a wide barrier, he once again returned to the heart of the blazing hell, retrieving, and relocating as many helpless animals as he could hold onto with each subsequent trip. After what seemed to be hours upon hours of conducting rescue mission after rescue mission, a final sweep seemed to confirm the endangered area was now clear of all wildlife. As he was about to breathe a long-awaited sigh of relief, he spotted a large bull elephant backed up against the wall of a steep ravine. He had nearly been overcome by smoke as a wall of fire raced across the dried grass directly toward him. T'Pal immediately dove downward, sweeping in ahead of the rapidly approaching wall of fire. Spreading his wings, he pressed the trapped elephant tightly against the earthen wall, shielding it from the flames with his own body. The fire was moving so quickly that within ten minutes it had completely passed their location, leaving nothing but scorched earth and ash in its wake.

When T'Pal lowered the fireproof shield of his wings, the final embers of the fire were already dying out as a wall of precipitation blew in from the west behind the lightning strike that originally ignited the blaze. The cool rain swept across the landscape like a broom, extinguishing the flames and the fears of the past twelve hours as life in the Serengeti slowly returned to normal.

T'Pal realized he was no closer to completing the challenge now than he had been upon leaving Adelaide to embark upon his mission. As he prepared to leave Africa for his journey back across the Indian Ocean, he noticed the bull elephant was still there, curiously staring at him.

Two hours later, T'Pal Mahajan descended into the roost of King Kai Bok Katari. The other prospective dragon kings were also there, but the anticipated collection of ivory tusks was quite conspicuously missing. All eyes were upon him as he lighted in their midst with the full-grown bull elephant comfortably in his grip.

There simply are not many things capable of moving dragons to laughter. In fact, most dragons are unsure of even *how* to laugh. Still, watching T'Pal enter the airspace over Adelaide with a full-grown bull elephant casually dangling from his claws, was indeed such an occasion. By the time they were safely on the ground, the entire group of dragons watching them were beside themselves with laughter.

"You said, bring two ivory tusks," stated T'Pal. "You never said they couldn't be attached to the elephant!" he added excitedly.

Having personally created the scenarios encountered by all four dragons, even King Kai Bok Katari had not remotely expected this result.

"T'Pal Mahajan, you have certainly achieved a most unexpected result," said the Southeastern Dragon King before asking, "How did you convince the elephant to come along with you?"

"I asked," answered T'Pal, matter-of-factly.

Smiling and shaking his head, King Kai Bok Katari said, "Well, I am probably just as curious as the rest of you, to hear King T'Aer Bolun Dakkar's evaluation of your individual outcomes."

As the collection of contenders prepared to take flight and return to The Himalayas, T'Pal Mahajan said, "Please excuse me, but I must return this magnificent specimen to his home in the Serengeti first; however, I should be along shortly."

"T'Pal, we are in Ahl Sha H'Araah," said King Kai Bok Katari. "There is no elephant to return."

As if awakening from a trance, all four contenders discovered they were now standing inside The King's Courtyard in the company of King J'Amal Aidin Kondur and the King of Kings, T'Aer Bolun Dakkar.

"Welcome, warriors all," said King J'Amal Aidin Kondur. "Once again, you have all performed admirably, this time, in completing the Ivory Challenge. During the challenge, each contender was forced to confront and overcome their primary weaknesses under the observation of King T'Aer Bolun Dakkar." Gesturing toward the King of Kings, he added, "It is he who will share the results of that evaluation."

Proudly looking over the valiant dragons before him, King T'Aer Bolun Dakkar said, "I could not have wished for a finer collection of aspiring dragon king ascendants. Each of you recognized the flaw in the challenge immediately, and none of you were tempted to take the life of such a noble creature or plunder its corpse. Although their blood is not of gold, desecrating the corpse of an elephant by removing its ivory is no different than pillaging the tombs of an ancestral dragon burial chamber. The true challenge was that of your abilities to face the unexpected obstacles that will invariably arise during the reign of a dragon king."

King T'Aer Bolun Dakkar approached K'Zahn D'Monicus first, saying, "Your strength lies within your drive to single mindedly accomplish tasks assigned to you. Your upbringing was an ongoing patchwork of demands by your father, Bokur D'Monicus, and your mother, Xiana Safir. As a dragon king, you will not be heeding the commands of others; you will be issuing and executing the responsibilities of a ruler, and the outcome of your decisions will be borne by your entire kingdom. When faced with the choice of ignoring the plights of others in pursuit of your own specific agenda, you did not hesitate. Instead of taking advantage of a situation that would have allowed you to easily acquire the coveted ivory tusks, you rushed to the defense of a soul who did not even realize his death was imminent. Not only did you prevent the death of that noble creature in full view of his offspring, you created a lasting deterrent for those who would have slain him, while injuring nothing but their pride."

Next, King T'Aer Bolun Dakkar turned to T'Aru Malka'Am to say, "Your ancestral lineage has born thousands of the fiercest warriors in the history of dragon-kind. Your legacy was forged in violence and destruction without regard for the lives lost on either side of a conflict. Your challenge was to show mercy, preserving lives as opposed to taking them. Even without the spoils of war or the praises sung of the victorious, the mercy you showed a mother, and her child were truly the acts of an honorable king. The Northeastern Dragon Kingdom would do well to have such an empathetic dragon king ascendant."

"J'Mir Mahajan," said King T'Aer Bolun Dakkar. "As a consummate diplomat, you have always sought solutions on a grand scale. You've allowed others to worry themselves with implementation of the resulting minutia while you basked in the individual glory of being the strategic architect. Your challenge was to focus on the needs of the one, without seeking the praise of the many. In accompanying an elderly elephant to his ancestral graveyard, you showed interest in his journey and displayed compassion for his plight. The simple act of protecting and comforting him through his final moments and giving him an honorable burial, far from the eyes of your diplomatic admirers, forced you not only to focus on the minutia, but also to get your hands dirty in the completion of it. As a dragon king, not all of your decisions will be popular, but they will be necessary. Today, you have risen to the occasion, understanding that each dragon deserves the attention of their king even when their needs are inherently confidential."

Finally, turning to T'Pal, King T'Aer Bolun Dakkar said, "A wise king should be deliberate in his decisions. His actions should naturally withstand the scrutiny of others, yet time is always a limited commodity. The depth of your considerations has always been both your most admirable trait and your most predictable weakness. An effective leader must often make decisions dynamically as crises develop around them. As a dragon king, you will never have the luxury of unlimited time. Just as in the challenge that confronted you in Ahl Sha H'Araah, decisions must often be made while you are actively attending to other issues that are just as urgent. With time, you will certainly develop a sense of prescience; however, time waits for no dragon and you must always take responsibility for your decisions, even those made in haste. T'Pal Mahajan, in the flames of the Serengeti, you acted as one would expect of a worthy dragon king, and somehow still found the time to consider returning an imaginary elephant."

T'Aer Bolun Dakkar's final comment to T'Pal, brought a sense of levity and relief to the warriors receiving his evaluations. In conclusion, he announced to the entire assembly of contenders, "You have all displayed the qualities of true dragon king ascendants, relying on your strengths while confronting and overcoming your weaknesses. It is with pride that I welcome each of you to the final challenge. We will reconvene here in the King's Courtyard in two days. Until then eat, rest, and be well."

Seconds later, Kings T'Aer Bolun Dakkar and J'Amal Aidin Kondur exited the arena into the tapestry of stars above.

CHAPTER 12

THE REASON FOR THE pause between challenges was simply to allow time for the contenders to reflect on their performance as well as the performances of their individual rivals. Deliberation is a key part of a dragon king's responsibilities because it allows them to consider and implement the best solutions for the matters at hand. While the need for immediate decisions is often unavoidable, whenever possible, a dragon king should take the time to weigh all sides of an issue before reaching his conclusions and implementing selected courses of action to address them.

While each prospective dragon king ascendant had successfully completed the tasks required to move on to the next challenge, there were also differing degrees of their successes to be considered before a final selection could be made. Completing a challenge did not necessarily mean the contenders had taken the best courses of action, but rather acceptable ones that met the established baseline requirements for advancement. The individual rankings and the effectiveness displayed by each of the four remaining challengers was currently the intellectual property of King T'Aer Bolun Dakkar and his bonded rider, Jake.

Jake and T'Aer Bolun Dakkar were both impressed with the remaining four dragons and justifiably so. They had all used wisdom, skill, and determination in completing their challenges, and their emotional growth was as obvious as was their determination. Unlike during the period preceding the first challenge, there was no detectable sense of false bravado or the assumption of superiority among them. In the course of a few short days, their focuses had shifted from the pursuit of their own desires for individual triumph, to firmly embracing behaviors that would be most beneficial to their kingdom.

With each challenge becoming progressively more and more difficult, the four remaining contenders were forced to reckon with the reality that ascendance to the throne was not an acknowledgement of personal victory. It was rather, a collective expression of hope by a kingdom that had placed their faith in a ruler to represent their best interests as a regional dragon community. While all of them were worthy, only one of them would ascend, setting the tone and ushering in a new era under a king who would rule for a thousand years.

"One question?" asked Jake as he and T'Aer Bolun Dakkar surfed Earth's upper atmosphere. "Are you certain that you can determine who will be the new dragon king ascendant with a single question?"

"It is not the question that will determine the future dragon king, but the answers to that question," responded T'Aer Bolun Dakkar. "Each of the four remaining contenders already knows the answer to the question I will ask, and lacking any other disqualifying factors, it is the one question that can accurately identify the most worthy dragon king ascendant."

"Well, I must agree that it will make the selection uncontestable," said Jake. "Still, the simplicity of the question is misleading and the mental gymnastics that will invariably accompany the decision-making process would be enough to drive both humans and dragons to the brink of insanity."

"As a dragon king, often the most consequential decisions will hinge on the simplest of questions," said T'Aer Bolun Dakkar. "History is not changed by a sudden deluge; it is polished gradually over time by the gentle current of a ceaseless stream. While many would prefer the grandeur of a single act that changes the path of history for the better, it will be a collection of simple, almost imperceptible actions that ultimately shape the future by gradually bending the arc of history over time. A dragon king will rule for a millennium, and during that time, this will be the question he will forever ask of himself, which is why I shall ask it of them all first."

Nodding with a smile, Jake said, "T'Aer Bolun Dakkar, I have known you for three-quarters of my life, and even with you taking up permanent residence inside my head, I still discover ways in which to be amazed by you."

"The feeling is mutual, dear Jake," said T'Aer Bolun Dakkar. "Still, for all of my accomplishments, I have yet to achieve the greatness reflected in the faces of your children, and each time I see them with Danni, it is clear to me there is no greater force of nature than that of a mother's love."

Jake and T'Aer Bolun Dakkar drifted introspectively through the night sky for another hour before returning to the idyllic paradise of Nin'Jahlah. In fewer than twenty-four hours, a single question would determine the dragon king ascendant for the most populous region of the planet. Before that, both the King of Dragon Kings and Jake, would rest prior to issuing their edict.

Throughout all four dragon kingdoms, speculation ran rampant as supporters for each of the contenders grew increasingly anxious to see which of the remaining dragons would be chosen to ascend. The anticipation was just as tangible in the three uncontested regions as it was in the Northeastern Dragon Kingdom. With virtually no dragons remaining neutral on the subject, support for each prospective dragon king ascendant was almost evenly split among K'Zahn D'Monicus, T'Aru Malka'Am, and J'Mir and T'Pal Mahajan. At this point, any of the four dragons in contention were more than qualified to ascend, and the vast majority of their supporters would unite behind whichever dragon was selected by King T'Aer Bolun Dakkar.

One particular dragoness known as Xiana Safir was of a very different opinion, and despite Bokur D'Monicus's unwillingness to participate in any further interference attempts, she had no intention of remaining on the sidelines when it came to stacking the odds in favor of her offspring, K'Zahn D'Monicus. Since Bokur D'Monicus would no longer submit to her demands, and no other dragons were willing to risk the consequences of being complicit in her schemes, Xiana Safir would need to take matters into her own hands.

It would be inaccurate to assume that male dragons were more deadly warriors than their female counterparts. Such an assumption would have no basis in fact and historical evidence would easily refute that conclusion. One of the deadliest dragons of all time was a seven-headed Hydra dragoness named L'Vira Khan. She was the primary purveyor of death to all who attempted to stand against the armies of her bonded rider, Genghis Khan. Her penchant for violence and destruction was so intense, the Mongolian Empire continued to grow even after Genghis Khan's death, until most of Eurasia had been conquered. Her reign of destruction lasted for nearly a century, until Toghan Temür Khan became paranoid of the powerful dragoness and plotted to destroy her. Instead, she turned against him, unleashing a plague known as the Black Death against the Mongols, killing nearly two-hundred-million people worldwide. In the end, it was King Tao Min Xiong who destroyed L'Vira Khan; the same dragoness that T'Arus D'Monicus had died trying to impress, during that final ill-fated Tournament of Dragons.

With the destruction of the ruthless L'Vira Khan, the Ming Dynasty was able to put an end to the Mongolian Empire; however, her century-long killing spree made her one of the deadliest dragons of all time, second only to Se'Thaa Malka'Am, the dragon who'd literally dragged an asteroid into the planet. Although Xiana Safir was no L'Vira Khan, she was certainly a formidable adversary, not to be taken lightly.

During the two-day rest and contemplation period before the final challenge, all the contenders remained isolated from everyone, unwilling to jeopardize their standing as potential dragon king ascendants. Even casual meetings between related dragons were prohibited. The only time they left their lairs was in order to feed on the bountiful fish swarms of the Indian Ocean. On the night before resuming the Conference of Kings, T'Pal Mahajan was en route to the oceanic feeding grounds. It was his first outing since the Ivory Challenge, and his mind was somewhat pre-occupied by self-critiquing past challenges while preparing for the upcoming one.

Xiana Safir had been stalking him from the moment he took to the skies. In her eyes, he was the apparent front-runner and therefore, the biggest obstacle between K'Zahn D'Monicus and his selection as dragon king ascendant to the throne of King J'Amal Aidin Kondur. Her plan was to attack and eliminate him in his weakened state before he could eat and replenish his energy. As he approached the teeming bait-ball swirling near the surface of the unusually placid waters, Xiana Safir descended rapidly, targeting the blind spot of a dragon focused on the meal in front of him. She was fewer than one hundred meters from her target when her carefully constructed plan seemed to go terribly awry.

Suddenly she was struggling to move as her wings were forcefully compressed to her sides and her body was restrained by the incredibly powerful constricting force that had instantly immobilized her in mid-flight. She struggled fiercely against the ever-tightening entanglement that was rapidly collapsing her airways and compressing her circulatory system to the point that her vision became compromised. Xiana Safir was disoriented and slowly lost consciousness, succumbing to the unbearable pressure squeezing the life from her, preventing the Hydra dragoness from even separating the necks upon which her six evil heads were perched. Her diminishing struggle gave way to darkness as the last strands of mental clarity abandoned her completely.

After devouring the enormous bait ball, T'Pal felt reinvigorated and ready to face the final challenge regardless of its nature. He returned to his lair, disappearing inside it without so much as a clue that he had been targeted by Xiana Safir, and with his stomach full and his mind clear, he fell into a deep uninterrupted sleep.

Hours later, with the sun turning the eastern horizon from black to light gray, Xiana Safir awoke somewhere in the snow-covered void between the dozens of nameless peaks within the Himalayan Mountain Range. There were deep gouges carved into the granite and thick metamorphic rock surrounding her, engraved by dragon claws more than capable of removing all six of her slumbering heads. Upon rising to her feet on wobbly legs, she recognized the unmistakable markings of Sirina Mahajan. Her long, serpent-like body had spiraled around Xiana Safir so quickly and so tightly, the Hydra dragoness had been unable to mount a defense of any kind. When she constricted, the pressure she exerted was so intense, the Naga Dragoness could easily have crushed the life from her six-headed adversary. The ragged gashes adorning the hard, stone surfaces upon which she had lain, were a not so gentle reminder to Xiana Safir, that T'Pal and J'Mir Mahajan, had a mother too.

CHAPTER 13

AT MIDNIGHT, KING T'AER BOLUN DAKKAR AND JAKE landed in the King's Courtyard. As expected, all four finalists were present under the watchful eyes of King J'Amal Aidin Kondur. Their excitement and curiosity were as obvious as their complete lack of trepidation regarding the challenge of King of Kings, T'Aer Bolun Dakkar.

"Good morning to all," said the king of dragon kings. "Our journey has been long, and the obstacles have been many, yet here you stand; all worthy, all capable, and all prepared to face the final challenge."

Each of the prospective dragon king ascendants had been puzzling over this particular challenge for the past two nights. With each advance, the challenges had grown progressively more complex, demanding ever-increasing levels of both physical and intellectual acuity in order to successfully navigate and complete them. Accordingly, each of the contenders anticipated a challenge requiring Herculean physical effort and razor-sharp instincts, and while they knew it would demand that they give their all, none among them seemed intimidated.

"Your final challenge is a question," said T'Aer Bolun Dakkar. "It is a question I have asked myself each day since King Tao Min Xiong named me as his dragon king ascendant, and now I ask it of you." Pausing briefly for effect, he asked, "If not you, then who?"

Lowering his wing, Jake swung back astride him as he said, "I will return for your answers in four hours." An instant later, they were gone.

After exchanging confused glances between them, the four contenders reluctantly left the arena. It did not take long for the magnitude of that single question to settle in on them. It was indeed a simple question, and it was clear why even the mighty T'Aer Bolun Dakkar would ask it of himself every single day. It was undeniable that each of the finalists had proven themselves during the course of the conference; however, would either of them be able to name one of their rivals to ascend in their stead?

The complexity of the situation expanded in the minds of each finalist like warming dough leavened with baker's yeast. The diversity of each possible answer and the potential ramifications of them were staggering in their complexity. If each dragon chose who they felt was the most unlikely candidate, hoping to receive more votes for themselves, that individual could be chosen to ascend. The same would apply to their perceived mid-tier candidate. The Mahajan brothers would understandably choose one another, even though it was the opinion of some that J'Mir was the weakest among them. The brutish T'Aru Malka'Am was a warrior born and bred with no royal lineage to speak of, and K'Zahn was the grandson of a traitor, but his integrity and leadership skills were above reproach. The contemplative T'Pal Mahajan was assumed by most, as likely to receive more votes of recognition than any other. Yet, in knowing this, others might refrain from selecting him for precisely that reason.

A logical option would be to answer the question honestly, naming the contender they truly felt would most faithfully serve the interests of the kingdom. There was no reason to assume that every dragon would view only one candidate as the likely ascendant. In fact, it was not beyond the realm of possibility to believe that each of the finalists would receive only a single vote.

Four hours to consider the myriad of options might just as well have been a lifetime. Each passing second brought deeper understanding for T'Aer Bolun Dakkar's ritual of daily self-evaluation. A dragon king must question every decision, both before and after making them. Whether they are exalted by the entire dragon kingdom or cursed by a single dragon within it, a king must live forever with decisions others are allowed to forget immediately. There are choices that need to be made and actions that need to be taken, and even when faced with impossible odds, a king must look beyond himself and be prepared to lead the charge. After all; if not him, then who?

Despite the breadth of the simple five-word question posed by King T'Aer Bolun Dakkar, all of the prospective dragon king ascendants arrived punctually, prepared to offer their responses. Additionally, all participants in the Conference of Kings had been invited and were in attendance along with the assembly of ruling dragon kings. After rejoining them in the King's Courtyard, the King of Kings summoned each dragon to him individually, beginning with K'Zahn D'Monicus. Next, he called forth J'Mir Mahajan, followed by T'Aru Malka'Am. Lastly, T'Pal Mahajan came forward to offer his answer before rejoining the other contenders in the arena.

Stepping forward, King T'Aer Bolun Dakkar first approached K'Zahn, saying, "K'Zahn D'Monicus, you have named T'Pal Mahajan."

Moving on to the next, he said, "T'Aru Malka'Am, you have named K'Zahn D'Monicus."

With the two heavily favored contenders already named, T'Aer Bolun Dakkar approached T'Pal, saying, "T'Pal Mahajan, you have named T'Aru Malka'Am."

With only one contender remaining, K'Zahn, T'Aru, and T'Pal, were all aware that J'Mir would be casting the final vote, effectively naming the future dragon king ascendant. As T'Pal's sibling, it was assumed by both K'Zahn D'Monicus and T'Aru Malka'Am, that he would most certainly choose his own blood over that of an outsider.

Finally, King T'Aer Bolun Dakkar approached and stood next to J'Mir, saying, "Of all gathered here, only one can be named the dragon king ascendant, and only one shall ascend to occupy the throne of the Northeastern Dragon Kingdom. The path of a dragon king is a lonely and demanding one with the weight of each decision falling squarely on the shoulders of a ruler who understands the journey before him." Turning to face the final contender, King T'Aer Bolun Dakkar said, "J'Mir Mahajan, you alone have understood and answered the question correctly, naming no one and assuming the weight of that enormous burden fully, realizing that in the end if *you* do not rise to meet the challenges facing the kingdom yourself, then no other dragon will be willing to accept you as their king."

Incredibly, K'Zahn D'Monicus, T'Aru Malka'Am, and T'Pal Mahajan, were all stunned; not by the selection of J'Mir Mahajan, but at the insightful wisdom of King T'Aer Bolun Dakkar. The question had been so simple, and yet so revealing. The obvious clue was in his admission to asking himself this very question each and every day. Why would a ruling king; the king of all dragon kings, ask of another that they execute his responsibilities? If not him, then who? As that elevated sense of wisdom sunk in, the acceptance of all three remaining contenders was unanimous.

Returning to his place among the other dragon kings, T'Aer Bolun Dakkar proudly exclaimed, "J'Mir Mahajan, it is with pride that we, the ruling dragon kings, name you as dragon king ascendant to the Northeastern Dragon Kingdom!"

The cheers of dragons erupting from the King's Courtyard could be heard resonating from the Crown of Earth and echoing across the snowy mountain peaks of the Himalayas from Nepal to the west, and into the heart of Tibet to the east. The congratulations offered by the numerous contestants in attendance were heartfelt and sincere, with J'Mir Mahajan graciously accepting them with the utmost humility.

In accordance with established tradition, after adjourning the Conference of Kings, there would be a full day of rest and reflection, followed by a flight of ascension in which King J'Amal Aidin Kondur and J'Mir Mahajan would circumnavigate the globe together, allowing the dragons of all regions to sense the new ascendants tug of familiarity.

With the gratitude of King J'Amal Aidin Kondur, King T'Aer Bolun Dakkar and Jake departed the King's Courtyard, taking in the scenery of the Crown of Earth one final time before heading south to feed in the Indian Ocean.

"Your insight never ceases to amaze me," said Jake to T'Aer Bolun Dakkar as they approached their targeted feeding area. "I honestly wasn't convinced that J'Mir Mahajan would be the one to answer the question correctly."

"It was simply a matter of logic," replied T'Aer Bolun Dakkar. "J'Mir Mahajan was the only contender who did not look to his rivals upon hearing the question. His eyes remained fixed on me, ignoring the scrutiny of his peers, even as they began comparing themselves to one another. As a dragon king, simply maintaining the status quo is the equivalent of losing in a world that marches ceaselessly forward. J'Mir was the only one who displayed the willingness to evolve beyond his own limitations, and in doing so, he was able to grasp the true essence of the question."

"It is not the role of the king to simply fit in," said Jake. "A king must lead, even if it means he must walk alone at times."

"Precisely," said T'Aer Bolun Dakkar. "Those afraid to leave the level path of convention will never reach the summit of their potential, for mediocrity has never been the cornerstone of greatness."

"Well said, dear friend," responded Jake. "If all my years spent bonded to you have taught me anything, it is not to fear the inevitability of change, for only through change can greatness be achieved."

As if on cue, T'Aer Bolun Dakkar and Jake plunged into the heart of the Indian Ocean, quickly corralling, and devouring an enormous school of herring before exiting the water and taking to the sky again. With merely a thought they vanished into the interdimensional rift of Ahl Sha H'Araah, reappearing seconds later over the unspoiled paradise of Nin'Jahlah.

Here, inside their secluded dimensional desert island, was the one place in all of creation they both hoped the inevitability of change, would leave undisturbed.

CHAPTER 14

IN THE HISTORY OF DRAGON KINGS, there had never been a time in which all four dragon kingdoms were simultaneously represented by bonded riders. Far more prevalent, were periods of time in which there were no liaisons between the worlds of dragons and humans whatsoever. Although King J'Amal Aidin Kondur had been bonded for nearly half a century, his rider had passed long before he was appointed by King Tao Min Xiong as ruler of the Northeastern Dragon Kingdom.

The selection of a new dragon king ascendant now made it possible to form a cooperative relationship between the leaders of dragon and human populations across Northern Africa and the Eurasian theater. The only missing element was a suitable candidate for the position.

King J'Amal Aidin Kondur had foreseen this opportunity and taken the preliminary steps necessary to identify receptive candidates. Just as King Tao Min Xiong had recognized Jake's potential long before pairing him with T'Aer Bolun Dakkar, the Northeastern Dragon King had already identified a handful of possible candidates for the eventual dragon king ascendant.

The vetting process for bonded riders is quite extensive and can last a dozen years or longer before the selected candidate is finally approached by their dragon. As with many things, Jake was the absolute exception to the rule. He had spotted and recognized T'Aer Bolun Dakkar for exactly what he was, nearly a decade earlier than planned; something previously considered to be impossible. As a result, their first encounter had been accelerated, creating an unprecedented and unusually powerful bond between them.

The candidates for bonded riders were often viewed as social outcasts by their contemporaries. They possessed qualities and skills that were often so pronounced, others felt uncomfortable around them despite acknowledging their intellectual brilliance. They were often labeled as autistic, mentally challenged, and reclusive, only because try as they might, they were unable to simplify their thoughts sufficiently for others to comprehend the information they were attempting to convey. With the passage of time, they grew deeply frustrated and withdrew even further into their emotional cocoons.

More often than not, they welcomed the vividly realistic dreams in which their dragons appeared to them, sharing their most exciting journeys and adventures with ever-increasing frequency. At the time of their first face-to-face meeting, most were already emotionally attached and able to greet their dragons by name.

Even though these gifted individuals were often identified during their pre-teen years, many of them would simply outgrow their affinity for dragons as they were swept along in the current of being a teenager. Such was the case with all but one of the candidates observed by King J'Amal Aidin Kondur. Her name was Aria Wong, and despite her families elevated social status, she was nearly invisible to them.

Her father, Michael Wong, was a veritable electronics kingpin in Singapore, having developed the production software for several manufacturing facilities located both domestically and abroad. Of three siblings, Aria was certainly the black sheep of the family, wanting nothing to do with the glitz and glamour of the high society so treasured by her brother, Steven, and her sister Cindy. She was much more comfortable spending long weekends with her grandfather in Kranji Countryside, far from the tall buildings and hyper-modern lifestyle of Singapore. There in the northwestern corner of the country surrounded by mangroves and farms, Aria's brilliant mind was unencumbered and able to explore the fanciful ideas and theories her siblings deplored, and her parents viewed as a complete waste of time. On the other hand, her grandfather always had an open mind and a willing ear for her, and remarkably, he shared her belief that dragons were real.

Now that a dragon king ascendant had been chosen, King J'Amal Aidin Kondur felt it was time to more clearly define the dragon who had routinely appeared in her dreamscape encounters. Before now, he had always been somewhat anonymous, with no specific identity or individualized countenance. With Aria's fifteenth birthday only a few weeks away, the time had come to give her dreams a face, and her dragon a name. Although their first direct encounter was still months if not years away, there was no reason to further delay a test of their emotional compatibility. By gradually introducing J'Mir Mahajan's specific details into the dreamscape encounters, their likelihood of developing a successful bond to one another could be more realistically gauged.

Aria Wong's mind automatically converted everything to numbers and then stored those numbers permanently. She could easily recall random strings of up to a thousand digits and then quickly reduce them to a single numeric value. She was also able to calculate the odds of something happening or not happening, then correctly choose the outcome of an event with unerring precision. To her father's delight, she could analyze his programming codes and determine their inaccuracies and inconsistencies almost instantly. However, to his great dismay, she had absolutely no interest in developing programming algorithms and would much rather occupy herself with the mathematical probability that dragons actually do exist.

Because of her unerring attention to detail, Aria was J'Mir Mahajan's ideal counterpart in the mind of J'Amal Aidin Kondur. J'Mir was a brilliant diplomat and a master when it came to strategic planning; however, precision was more of a loose concept to him rather than a hard and fast rule. By working together, their combined strengths would effectively eliminate their individual weaknesses to the benefit of both human and dragon societies.

Late that evening, Aria found herself standing outside her grandfather's farmhouse walking toward the barn, several hundred feet from the front door. Despite not realizing how she'd gotten there, she continued to the barn without even looking back. There was an uneasiness among the animals inside that couldn't really be described as fear. It felt more like they were children hiding a friend who had run away from home. Slowly walking past the stalls of goats and Falabella miniature horses, she noticed two glowing golden eyes standing out from the dark shadows at the back of the structure. Surprisingly, her curiosity far outweighed her fear as she approached the dark recesses, stopping just outside the unnatural wall of near-absolute darkness.

When she slowly extended her arm, her hand literally vanished upon breaching the black barrier that completely swallowed any light attempting to pierce it. On the other side of the opaque divider, she felt the warm soft face of what was obviously a horse. It was certainly not one of her grandfather's goats or miniature Falabella horses. She knew all of them by name and they would never attempt to conceal themselves from her.

"Who are you?" she asked, calmly caressing the horse's nose and softly flaring nostrils. "You don't have to be afraid."

From the darkness, the horse slowly opened its eyes, once again revealing the golden glow that had originally caught her attention. The veil of darkness surrounding him evaporated like the final remnants of fog touched by warm sunlight. She recognized the animal immediately, saying, "You are a Przewalski's horse. How on Earth did you ever get here?"

"I wanted to meet you," replied J'Mir Mahajan.

Aria was not the least bit shocked at the notion of having a conversation with the horse. The aura surrounding them felt natural and comforting, as if they had known each other since the beginning of time.

"You wanted to meet me?" asked Aria. "You're obviously a long way from home. Why would you travel such a great distance to meet me?"

"I would have traveled even farther had it been necessary," said J'Mir Mahajan. "You are more special than even King J'Amal Aidin Kondur described," he added.

"You know a king?" asked Aria, curiously.

"I know four of them," replied the horse, enjoying the gentle hand that continued to stroke is face. "And they all know you."

Smiling, Aria asked, "Why would even a single king be interested in a farmgirl like me; let alone, four of them?"

"Because they have already seen what I have just now discovered," replied J'Mir Mahajan. "You are perfect."

"My family might be inclined to disagree with you," said Aria with a hint of sadness temporarily clouding her face. "They think that I'm mentally unstable, although they are far too polite to say those words out loud where others might hear them." Looking into the horse's eyes, she added, "That's why they are so happy when I choose to spend time with my grandfather on this secluded farm."

"Your father is one of Singapore's most successful businessmen," said J'Mir. "The expectations placed on his shoulders unfortunately spill over onto those surrounding him." With his gaze directly meeting hers, he said, "Your family loves you deeply, but they do not understand you deeply. They search for meaning beneath them when your brilliance is far above their heads."

"What shall I call you, Mr. Przewalski's horse?" asked Aria as a faint smile returned to her lips.

"I am J'Mir Mahajan," he answered.

"Will you stay here with me, J'Mir Mahajan?" queried the young woman.

"This is only a dream, Aria Wong," replied J'Mir. "Neither of us can remain here. When you awaken in the morning, you will not even remember our dreamscape conversations, but they will continue to exist beyond the limits of consciousness."

"But why?" asked Aria, already saddened at the thought of missing him. "You are my only friend."

"This is necessary to prevent you from losing sight of reality and succumbing to the temptation of forever remaining inside the dream," answered J'Mir. "You must eat and grow and learn and exist in the realm of reality. In centuries past, humans have actually died in their sleep, unwilling and unable to awaken from the allure of their dreamscapes."

"Will you at least visit me here again," asked Aria, already at the verge of tears.

"Not only will I visit you in your dreams," replied J'Mir. "I will watch over you when you awaken, and even if you feel that you are alone against the world, you will no longer be."

As J'Mir began to step back into the shadows, Aria threw her arms around his neck, hugging him with her eyes shut tightly.

"Aria. Wake up sleepyhead," said a voice, tugging her back from her enchanting reverie. When she opened her eyes, her grandfather was sitting on the edge of the bed smiling down at her. "Would you like to help me with the horses this morning?" he asked.

Nodding excitedly, Aria sprang from the bed and quickly dressed. After pulling on her rubber boots and tucking her pants into them, she darted out the door making a beeline for the barn. As always, the baby goats and miniature Falabella horses were excited to see her as she fed them with an unexplainable new enthusiasm. At the back of the barn, she hesitated only for a moment as if expecting to see someone or something there. Finding nothing, she joyfully went about the remainder of her morning chores before joining her grandfather for breakfast in the farmhouse dining room.

When they had finished eating, she collected the plates and utensils, carrying them over to the kitchen sink. Pausing for a moment, she asked, "Opa, have you ever seen a Przewalski's horse before?"

"When I was younger," he answered. "In Mongolia where I grew up, there were still a few of them roaming wild, but that was nearly fifty... No, sixty years ago." Eying her curiously, he said, "Why do you ask?"

"I'm not really sure," Aria replied. "It just happened to cross my mind, I guess."

After finishing the dishes and putting them away, she asked, "Can we get one?"

"Get one?" asked her grandfather, curiously. "Get one what?"

"A Przewalski's horse." answered Aria. "I think that would be lovely."

Her grandfather had to smile. He loved her colorful imagination and was always delighted at her fanciful ideas and inquiries. "I thought you wanted a dragon," he said, unable to curb his desire to chuckle out loud."

"I do," said Aria, her eyes growing wide with excitement. "I think we should have both!"

Nodding and attempting to light the antique Meerschaum pipe clutched between his teeth, he offered, "How about we work on finding your dragon first. After that, we'll see about finding a Przewalski's horse for you."

"That would be wonderful!" exclaimed Aria, rushing over to hug her beloved grandfather before darting toward the door. Before leaving the house, she lingered, turning to him again to say, "Thank you Opa. I love you." A second later, she was dashing down the porch steps toward the barn to play with the farm animals.

Watching her through the kitchen window as she bounded off, her grandfather thought to himself, "*A mythological creature or an extinct horse. If anyone deserves to find either of them; it's Aria.*"

CHAPTER 15

AS HAD BEEN THE CASE with T'Aer Bolun Dakkar and every other dragon king ascendant before him, contact with the king currently occupying the throne to which J'Mir Mahajan would ascend, was highly irregular. After their joint flight of ascension, their only contact would occur during dreamscape scenarios scripted by King J'Amal Aidin Kondur to prepare J'Mir for his role as king.

This period of separation was essential in maintaining the sovereignty of the current king and avoiding the perception that his edicts could be challenged or circumvented in any way. Until J'Amal Aidin Kondur relinquished his kingdom to J'Mir Mahajan in the final minutes of his life, his rule remained absolute and unquestionable.

Likewise, J'Mir Mahajan, having proven himself as champion during the Conference of Kings, would remain unchallengeable until he assumed the mantle of the Northeastern Dragon King. This period of immunity allowed him the opportunity to expand his knowledge, increase his strength and battle skills, and in this case, build upon and intensify the connection to his chosen bonded rider.

The mental isolation of Aria Wong from her dreamscape encounters with J'Mir Mahajan allowed her to resume her normal life without the comingling of realities. Nevertheless, the resulting evolution of her character and self-confidence unquestionably carried over into her physical reality. Her brother and sister noticed those gradual changes first. Although she retained her somewhat quirky character traits, she no longer seemed to be ashamed of, or embarrassed by them. To the contrary, she embraced her highly unusual skill set with renewed vigor, sailing through her advanced algebra, trigonometry, calculus, and topology classes, and integrating those skills into her physics studies as if they were all child's play.

By her eighteenth birthday, she had either created or "corrected" nearly every software program used by her father's manufacturing clients in factories around the world. Even though her father listed her work as the intellectual property of Wong Electronic Innovations (WEI-Singapore), it didn't take long for his competition to recognize the goose laying those billion-dollar golden eggs for his company.

It wasn't unusual for WEI-Singapore to receive threats against their board of directors, or even against Michael Wong, himself. In fact, most companies dealing in billion-dollar contracts and worldwide software applications consider them to be a normal part of doing business on such a grand scale. The complex, multi-layered security protocols established to protect the senior corporate directors at WEI-Singapore were more than exhaustive, costing the company well in excess of two billion dollars per year; merely

a drop in the bucket of a company boasting a trillion-dollar net worth.

Despite their confidence in the beyond state-of-the-art security apparatus that had kept them safe for many years, when Michael Wong's personal secretary received the call from Leung Fu, wishing to make an appointment, even WEI-Singapore's chief security coordinator was extremely concerned. Leung Fu was rumored to be the undisputed head of the Fu Triad operating from Hong Kong, and a personal appointment with him was the last thing anyone wanted.

Although Michael Wong had no interest in connections to any brokers of organized crime, not taking the appointment request from Leung Fu would be perceived as both an insult and a sign of weakness. Against the advice of his security chief and the gnawing discomfort in his gut, Michael Wong granted the appointment request for the following week. With several days to prepare and add extra layers of security to their existing protocols, he felt confident Leung Fu's visit would pose no significant threat to him or his company.

Jake got word of the appointment through his back-channel information network in Taiwan. Since there had been no dedicated bonded rider for the Northeastern Dragon Kingdom for centuries, Jake and Danni had been working with King J'Amal Aidin Kondur, serving as liaisons for the region. Normally, they had no interest in the inner workings of the triads as long as their disputes didn't negatively affect the delicate balance of the Asian oceanic ecosystems. Although Jake was well aware of the industries either controlled or extorted by the Fu Triad, he had neither a reason nor a desire to interfere in the regional politics and economic traditions of China or Singapore. That all changed the moment the name Aria Wong was mentioned as a potential point of leverage by one of Leung Fu's highest-ranking lieutenants.

Jake and T'Aer Bolun Dakkar had observed the young woman during her interactions with J'Mir Mahajan on numerous occasions. They used the information collected over the course of many years, to shape dreamscape scenarios that prepared both J'Mir and Aria for the important work they would assume when J'Mir Mahajan ascended to the throne as Northeastern Dragon King. Unfortunately, it was still months too soon for their official introduction outside the dreamscape scenarios, and until such time, real-world interactions between J'Mir and Aria would need to be strictly avoided.

Unlike Aria, J'Mir retained the memories of their encounters both inside and outside the dreamscape scenarios. They remained as vivid for him during his waking hours as they had been inside the dreams. Just as T'Aer Bolun Dakkar had invisibly hovered over Jake for years before their initial meeting, J'Mir was never far from Aria. He was her guardian by day and her mentor by night, but the type of intervention needed to protect her from the Fu Triad would require an elevated level of involvement that neither of them were prepared to deal with.

Were anyone to pose a threat to Aria, J'Mir would most assuredly overreact. Although Aria loved J'Mir inside the realm of dreamscapes that were inaccessible during her waking hours, J'Mir loved her always, whether he was dreaming or not. Should anyone harm, or even threaten to harm her, J'Mir would unleash a reign of terror over them that would obliterate the carefully maintained veil of separation between humans and dragons.

To prevent such a carnival of horrors, Jake and T'Aer Bolun Dakkar would intervene on their behalf. After informing J'Mir Mahajan of both the threat and their plan of action and ensuring him that no harm would come to either Aria or her family, J'Mir reluctantly agreed not to interfere.

Three days later, Leung Fu entered the impenetrable vault of his lavish Hong Kong office. Casually flipping through the incoming texts on his iPhone, he took a seat behind the ornately carved teak desk that dominated the office space like the throne of an ancient emperor. He had already been seated there for several minutes before he noticed the silhouette of a man sitting nonchalantly in one of the upholstered leather chairs at the far wall of his office. Without looking up, he calmly reached beneath the desk, flipping the toggle-switch located there.

"You can keep flipping it until it breaks off," said Jake, stepping out of the shadows with Turbo casually draped over his right forearm. "No one is coming."

"Jacob Payne," said Leung Fu, his voice dripping with sarcasm. "To what do I owe this unexpected pleasure?"

"It seems we have overlapping interests," answered Jake.

"Overlapping interests?" queried Leung Fu. "I have no dealings outside our agreed-upon drilling zones, and we are well within our quarterly catch volumes in the Indian Ocean. I see no overlap in our interests."

"I do appreciate the fact that you have honored our agreements, and hopefully you will continue to do so," said Jake. "I'm sure the patents for the desalination and water purification filters I've given you, will continue to serve your financial interests far into the future."

"Indeed, they will," replied Mr. Fu. "So, what can I do for you this morning, Mr. Payne?"

"Aria Wong," said Jake. "Whatever dealings you have with her father, do not concern her and I ask that you omit her from any negotiations or leveraging attempts concerning WEI-Singapore."

"You are far from our established boundaries, Mr. Payne," said Leung Fu. "I have no interest in overfishing or drilling in delicate ecosystems, and the profits from the water filtration systems makes such unsightly endeavors wholly superfluous. However, the software and programming industries do not fall within the boundaries of our agreement. I see no need for your permission in determining my negotiation tactics."

"I am simply asking, man to man, that you do not attempt to use Aria or any of Michael Wong's family as leverage. She is of great personal value to me, and by extension, so is her family," said Jake. "I am certain that two honorable businessmen like you and Michael Wong, can reach an agreement that does not involve threats against Aria or her family."

"And this great personal value that you speak of; how deeply are you willing to invest in maintaining it?" asked Leung. "Make me an offer."

"I will not trade one form of blackmail for another," said Jake. "This would be more of a gentlemen's agreement."

"Blackmail is such an ugly word, Mr. Payne. I'm insulted that you would accuse me of such a thing inside my own office," said Leung. "A gentlemen's agreement wouldn't require such an insinuation."

"The gentlemen's agreement is simply my way of telling you beforehand, that if you so much as disrupt her daily routine in even the smallest of ways, the Fu family will cease to be the region's controlling triad before the sun sets on that very same day," said Jake without so much as furrowing his brow.

"And why should I even believe you are capable of carrying out such a threat? You may have paid off someone to gain access to my inner sanctum. No matter. I will find him and kill him," said Leung Fu. "There is, however, the small matter of you leaving this room, to say nothing of the building Mr. Payne, and a lot of things can happen between the 108th floor and the lobby."

"There is no one to kill, Mr. Fu," said Jake. "I needed no one's help to get in, and your lobby full of assassins will not prevent me from leaving."

There was no accounting for the time it took for Jake to cross the thirty-foot expanse between them and grip Leung Fu by the front of his ridiculously expensive suit jacket. Carrying him across the room with his shoes a full meter above the floor, Jake literally slammed Leung into the two-foot thick ballistic distortion glass overlooking Hong Kong.

The speed at which everything transpired left Leung dazed and completely disoriented. When he opened his eyes, the charming face of the world-renowned Jacob Payne was unrecognizable to him. The complete lack of emotion and the vacant look in Jake's eyes reminded Leung of a Jiangshi; a demonic mix between a zombie and a vampire, sent to rip the tainted soul from his body. The eyes of the tiny chihuahua casually perched on Jake's forearm were also staring up into his, with what appeared to be boiling gold swirling inside them.

"I will make no further requests," growled Jake. "There will be no threats, discussions of leverage, or submission to your attempts at blackmail. If you visit the offices of WEI-Singapore, you will do so as a businessman, or you will cancel your appointment due to unforeseen circumstances."

Slowly sliding Leung Fu down the window until his feet touched the floor, Jake said, "You are officially, no longer untouchable. Either here inside your treasury vault of an office, in the fortified bunker twenty meters beneath your fortress of a home, or while traveling in your caravan of armored vehicles; if I want you, I will get to you!"

Smoothing out the front of Leung's crinkled suit jacket for him, Jake once again looked as if he had come to Mr. Fu's office for a photo shoot with his tiny accessory dog perched decoratively on his arm. "Aria Wong and her family are off limits," said Jake. "Chant that mantra to yourself non-stop until it sinks in," he added, turning to walk towards the veritable vault of an office door. Before they reached it, both Jake and Turbo vanished into thin air.

CHAPTER 16

TWO DAYS AFTER Jake's and Turbo's trip to Hong Kong, Leung Fu called Michael Wong's personal secretary, informing her that he would not be able to keep their scheduled appointment. Evidently, an important family matter had unexpectedly arisen, and he would need to attend to it personally. Before she could ask if he would like to reschedule, he terminated the call abruptly and never called back. Michael Wong and his entire security team were incredibly relieved, and none of them ever spoke of the cancelled appointment or brought up the incident again.

Six months later, Aria's grandfather received a call from Jacob Payne. He'd heard of Shen Wong's farm in Kranji Countryside and was hoping Mr. Wong would agree to harbor one of his most prized animals. Although Jake didn't reveal the specific details, by the time he arrived at Mr. Wong's farm, Aria had already told him about Jacob Payne in great detail. In fact, she'd raved on and on about him for days, and when Jake's rental vehicle finally turned onto the long driveway leading up to his house, he felt as if they'd been friends for a lifetime.

Exiting the large SUV towing a horse trailer, he approached the farmer with and extended hand and a wide, sincere smile, saying, "Mister Wong, I'm Jacob Payne, and it is such a pleasure to finally meet you!"

"The honor is all mine, Mister Payne," replied Mister Wong. "Please, call me Shen."

"Thank you, Shen," Jake replied. "And please call me Jake."

As the two of them walked around to the back of the trailer, Jake explained, "I apologize for the secrecy surrounding my visit, but you seem to be one of only a handful of men who have any experience with a horse like this, and I was hoping I could entrust him to you."

"I appreciate your confidence in me, Jake," said Shen Wong, expecting to find another miniature Falabella inside the trailer. "I'm sure Aria and I will be able to provide a great home for him," he added, waving Aria over to join them."

"Hello, Mister Payne!" said a smiling Aria, trying hard to contain her excitement. "I have heard so much about you!"

"Well, it's wonderful to meet you, and I hope it won't be too much of an imposition to leave him in your care."

After opening the side door near the horse's head, Jake stepped aside to allow Shen and Aria and unobstructed view of the golden-eyed Przewalski's horse waiting patiently in the trailer. Shen stepped back, dropping his Meerschaum pipe to the ground as his eyes widened in utter disbelief. As if in a trance, Aria held out her hand walking slowly toward the magnificent horse. Drawing nearer, she closed her eyes, whispering to herself, "Please don't disappear. Please don't disappear. Please don't disappear."

Suddenly, she felt her hand press against his face, and while holding it there, she slowly opened her eyes. Unlike in her dreams, this time he did not vanish. "I know you," she said with a smile. "We've met before, haven't we?"

The horse nodded in the affirmative while softly neighing.

"How did you...? Where did you...? How is this even possible?" stammered Shen Wong. "This is a Przewalski's horse! I thought they were extinct and If I weren't staring directly at him with my own eyes, I would not even believe it to be possible!"

"He is truly a rare specimen," said Jake, picking up Shen's pipe and handing it back to him. "Perhaps even the last of his kind, and much to special to be put on display as some zoo attraction." Looking at Aria, he said, "I believe he will be in very good hands with you."

"Yes," replied Aria. "I will protect him with my very life if I have to."

"Of that, I have no doubt," said Jake. "Should you need anything—anything at all,"

"No," interjected Aria. "He will want for nothing."

When Jake lowered the ramp at the rear of the trailer, Aria guided the horse out and led him into the barn without either a rope or bridle. He simply followed her as if he knew where they were going.

Shen Wong invited Jake inside for tea, and Turbo hopped out of the truck, following Aria and her horse into the stable. He watched from a distance as she held the horse's face in her hands, pressing her forehead against his. The two of them remained frozen in that position for several minutes while three years of dreamscape encounters became reality for Aria, just as they had always been for J'Mir.

The sun had already set when Jake and Shen Wong came outside again. Aria and J'Mir remained inside the stable as Turbo trotted out of the barn to rejoin Jake and Shen at the truck.

"It has been a pleasure getting to know you, Shen," said Jake, firmly shaking his hand. "If there is anything, I can do for you; anything at all, please don't hesitate to call on me."

"Jake, you have fulfilled one of my granddaughter's greatest wishes," Shen replied. "If there is ever anything that I can do for you, I would consider it an honor."

Looking toward the barn, Shen started to call out to Aria, but Jake interrupted him, saying, "No. Let them get acquainted. It's not every day that two such kindred spirits find each other. Please allow them as much time together as they need."

"Thank you, Jake," said Shen as he watched the humble billionaire climb into the rented SUV with his tiny canine companion. Moments later, they turned onto the main road headed back to Singapore City.

Before heading inside for the evening, Shen Wong walked over to the barn where a single light bulb illuminated the area outside the large formerly vacant stable at the far end of the building. Approaching quietly, he peered over the door where he saw Aria and the Przewalski's horse both asleep in the deep straw covering the floor of the stable. Removing a large blanket from a nearby shelf, he covered both of them before turning off the light and quietly walking back toward the front of the barn. At the door, he paused briefly, thinking he'd noticed the faint scent of burning flesh before realizing it was probably just an odd combination of his pipe tobacco and the earthy smells inside the barn. Smiling to himself, he closed the barn door and walked back up to the house.

After returning the rental vehicle and trailer to the dealership in Singapore City, Jake and T'Aer Bolun Dakkar took to the sky. The tiny island nation quickly vanished in the distance as they rapidly took on altitude.

While basking in the silence of Earth's upper atmosphere, Jake said, "It seems like only yesterday that I was nearly crashing into you on my bicycle. Now, Aria Wong and J'Mir Mahajan are about to embark on the same wonderful journey that brought us to this point."

"Hopefully, they will make the time to view the world from this perspective often," said T'Aer Bolun Dakkar. "It seems that the closer you are to the surface, the more difficult it becomes to see the purpose of our work."

"How could they not?" asked Jake. "I can still vividly recall our first flight together. I was terrified until I felt the rush of the wind in my face and the inseparable bond that reassured me you would never abandon me. That's when I realized I had never been afraid of flying. I'd been afraid of falling. You took that fear from me and in an instant, I was free."

"We all have our own fears to overcome," said T'Aer Bolun Dakkar. "Your fear was of falling, and my fear was of failing. Just as I did not let you fall; you did not let me fail."

"I couldn't let you fail," said Jake. "Everyone expected that of us because I was too young, and you were the privileged offspring of the legendary King Tao Min Xiong. The odds were stacked against us from the very beginning, but you, T'Aer Bolun Dakkar; you believed in me. I could do no less for you."

"Now, we must prepare J'Mir Mahajan and Aria Wong for the challenges they will certainly face upon ascending to the throne of the Northeastern Dragon Kingdom," said T'Aer Bolun Dakkar. "Xiana Safir is not yet satisfied with the outcome of the Conference of Kings. She will wait for the passing of King J'Amal Aidin Kondur before she coerces and cajoles one of her sons to challenge J'Mir Mahajan. I suspect it will be Mi'Kah D'Monicus who answers her call."

"I agree," said Jake. "She has lost her maternal influence over Na'Desh D'Monicus, and K'Zahn D'Monicus will undoubtedly respect the outcome of the Conference of Kings."

"Yes," said T'Aer Bolun Dakkar. "Having survived the battle challenge against Danang for nearly fifty hours longer than J'Mir Mahajan, Mi'Kah D'Monicus most likely feels confident that he can successfully challenge and defeat the new king in battle."

"Then we must be diligent in our preparations," said Jake. "Although we cannot fight J'Mir Mahajan's battles for him, it is incumbent upon us to ensure he is ready to take on all challengers beginning from his very first hour as king."

"Then ready he shall be," replied King T'Aer Bolun Dakkar before disappearing with Jake into the interdimensional rift of Ahl Sha H'Araah.

The next morning, Shen Wong was surprised to find Aria had already prepared breakfast for him when he came into the dining room.

"It seems that someone slept well in the stables last night," said Shen with a smile.

"He is so amazing, Opa," said Aria. "It's like heaven made him just for me!"

"Well, apparently that is true," said Shen. "Jake told me, he may even be the last Przewalski's horse on the planet, and somehow, he found his way to our doorstep."

"They say that if you wish hard enough for something, destiny will eventually bring it to you," said Aria.

"Then I guess we'd better get to work clearing out another stall," said Shen. "We're going to need it for your dragon."

Smiling thoughtfully, Aria said, "You know, Opa; I think we're good." Staring out the window at the Przewalski's horse grazing comfortably in the pasture behind the barn, she softly repeated, "Yep. I think we're good."

CHAPTER 17

EVEN AFTER THREE YEARS of dreamscape scenarios and battles, there is still nothing that compares to the nervous anticipation of one's first flight with a dragon.

"Are you sure I won't fall off?" asked Aria.

"That would be quite impossible," replied J'Mir Mahajan. "But, if you do, I will catch you."

Lightly tapping her shoulder with a razor-sharp talon was all it took for Aria's armor to self-deploy. As a comforting warmth began to spread through her entire body, she looked down to find she was covered from head to toe in the exact same layered scales as J'Mir Mahajan. With the emergence of her armor, her fear of flying instantly dissipated, and she could not wait to climb aboard.

J'Mir Mahajan lowered his left wing and she swung astride, taking a comfortable seat just in front of his wings. The way their armors instantly meshed upon contact gave Aria the extra boost of confidence she needed, and only a few seconds later, they were nearly a mile above their tiny farm and the tiny little island nation of Singapore.

"This is even more amazing than I imagined!" screamed Aria into the wind whipping past them.

"There is no need to scream," said J'Mir Mahajan. "Our thoughts are as tightly connected as is our armor," he added.

"I know," screamed Aria even louder. "But this is so amazing!"

J'Mir Mahajan soared into the blackness of the night sky above them, looping and spiraling as they approached the edge of the stratosphere, then steeply descended again towards the glowing blue orb of Earth below. Aria's confidence bloomed completely when she realized, everything she had experienced during her dreamscapes was now possible in her reality.

After being airborne for nearly an hour, J'Mir Mahajan said, "There is someone I would like for you to meet."

"Whoever you'd like me to," Aria replied. "I trust you completely."

Shortly thereafter, they were landing in the barren expanse of the Sahara Desert, surrounded by nothing but sand and starlight. A few yards away from them, she noticed the silhouette of a large man standing at the top of one of the dunes, framed by a diamond-like back drop of stars. As they drew nearer, she realized that it was Jacob Payne and the tiny little chihuahua that had accompanied him to their farm.

"Mr. Payne!" she said excitedly. "What are you doing way out here in the middle of nowhere?"

"I just wanted to check on you to make sure you and J'Mir were doing alright," replied Jake with a smile.

"But... How did you get way out here?" Aria asked.

"We have a lot more in common than you think," said Jake. "In one year, J'Mir Mahajan will ascend to the throne of the Northeastern Dragon Kingdom, and you will ascend with him. I will be your mentor for the next few months to help you prepare for his ascension."

"I don't quite understand," said Aria. "What do I need to do?"

"You will need to improve your flight coordination and battle skills," answered Jake. "J'Mir is already quite a formidable warrior; however, as a dragon king, he must be ready to defend his right to the throne immediately upon ascending. As his bonded rider, you must be prepared to engage any and all challengers alongside him. It is my responsibility to make sure both of you are ready to face and defeat them."

"But how can you train us to fight up there, from down here?" asked Aria, looking up into the stars.

"I brought my own ride," said Jake, placing Turbo on the ground in front of him. T'Aer Bolun Dakkar immediately unfolded, towering above everything, seeming to blot out half the stars in the heavens. "This is King T'Aer Bolun Dakkar, and together, we will be your trainers, your allies, and your loyal friends."

Aria was staring upward in amazement, unable to believe her eyes. The tiny dog she had all but overlooked when they visited her grandfather's farm, was now dwarfing the surrounding dunes and bathing them in darkness.

Her thoughts were an array of numbers, statistics, probability calculations, and uncharted theories in physics. She boiled all of that down to four syllables, asking, "When do we start?"

"Immediately!" replied Jake, donning his armor, and climbing up the lowered wing of T'Aer Bolun Dakkar with catlike agility. "Follow us!" said Jake, as he and the enormous dragon launched into the sky.

Aria and J'Mir Mahajan were right behind them as the four of them disappeared into the star-studded galactic masterpiece above the vastness of the Sahara. For the rest of the night and into the wee hours of the morning, the four of them sliced through the skies of Northern Africa. J'Mir and Aria mimicked the aerial acrobatics of T'Aer Bolun Dakkar and Jake, doing their best to keep up with them although it was clear Jake's dragon was not even close to the limits of his abilities.

Aria had never met anyone who could think as quickly as she could. Not only was Jake's mind as sharp as hers, but he also developed and initiated these complex and unpredictable flight and attack patterns on the fly, while she strained to anticipate and plot them as mathematical equations in her mind.

Shortly before dawn, Aria and J'Mir quietly landed in the pasture behind the barn. Despite their extreme exhaustion, they were satisfied at their first night of training by the most skilled dragon and rider duo to have ever ruled the skies. It would take days for Aria to digest the trigonometry behind the geometrically insane angles and attack vectors rapidly developed by Jake, and instantaneously acted upon by T'Aer Bolun Dakkar. By the time Shen softly knocked on her bedroom door later that morning, there were numbers and calculations and asymmetrical geometric patterns written and drawn on dozens of sheets of paper taped to the walls, floor, and ceiling of the room.

"I thought you could calculate everything in your head," said Shen, openly astonished at the all-encompassing project she was working on.

"I did too," said Aria. "Obviously, I was mistaken."

"Well, I've never seen you *this* absorbed in anything involving math," said Shen.

"This is so much more than mathematics, Opa. This is the real-world application of the theories and program algorithms I've been studying and creating for my father for the past ten years. Compared to... all of this," said Aria, gesturing toward the dozens of calculations and drawings adorning every available surface of her room. "Everything else was like coloring with crayons!"

Stepping back from her visually perplexing handiwork, Aria said, "Breakfast is ready, and I've made us some tea. I need to take a break anyway."

"It's six o'clock in the morning!" exclaimed Shen. "How long have you been working on this... project?" he added, gesturing around the room.

"Only a couple of hours, but I wanted to write it all down while it was still fresh in my mind," answered Aria, smiling as she walked past Shen and down the hallway to the kitchen, where she plated and served the breakfast she'd prepared for them earlier.

Smiling at her from across the breakfast table, Shen couldn't help but be amazed. During the past year, he had watched her grow from a bashful but curious little girl, to a brilliant, self-confident young woman. It was as if that golden-eyed Przewalski's horse Jake had given them, had somehow unlocked a part of her personality that was longing for a challenge. Clearly, she'd found it.

For five years, Xiana Safir had been brooding. She blamed Bokur, Na'Desh, and K'Zahn D'Monicus for not taking the steps necessary to install one of her offspring as King of the Northeastern Dragon Kingdom. The constant stream of complaints from her six nonsensical heads were all directed to the ears of Mi'Kah

D'Monicus. Despite his attempts to tune them out, their ceaseless stream of victimization claims was like a torrent of guilt pouring from her mouths in an ever-flowing fountain of grievances.

Na'Desh was the pitiful son who had abandoned her. K'Zahn was the stupid son who had disappointed her. Bokur was the ungrateful mate who had always been unworthy of her. How could she have been surrounded by so many useless and incompetent dragons?

"Fortunately, I have one brave and loyal son!" she would constantly say to Mi'Kah. "Of all my sons, only you truly love and understand me."

With each passing day, her symphony of injustices became louder and more insistent, until even the final fragments of Mi'Kah D'Monicus's self-esteem had been completely eroded away. After months of emotional bombardment, Mi'Kah was beaten down to the point where he would do anything, she asked of him, if only she would be silent!

As a means of escaping her toxic presence, even if merely for a short time, Mi'Kah D'Monicus trained and honed his battle skills for hours upon hours each day. During that time, he would redirect his rage and frustration to the avatar he faced inside the transitional dimension of Ahl Sha H'Araah; the avatar of J'Mir Mahajan. If he needed to take down a dragon king in order to end this madness, then that was precisely what he would do.

CHAPTER 18

KING J'AMAL AIDIN KONDUR summoned J'Mir Mahajan to him on the first day of winter. Just as J'Mir and Aria, T'Aer Bolun Dakkar and Jake also felt the tug of familiarity coursing through them.

"It is time," said T'Aer Bolun Dakkar. "Tonight, a great king passes, and a new king will ascend with his bonded rider."

"King J'Amal Aidin Kondur will be deeply missed," said Jake. "J'Mir Mahajan and Aria Wong will have a large shadow to fill."

"They are ready," replied T'Aer Bolun Dakkar. "They have grown stronger, both as individuals and as a team. The Northeastern Dragon Kingdom will be in competent hands."

Not long after sensing the pulse, J'Mir and Aria joined King J'Amal Aidin Kondur near his roost in the Himalaya Mountain Range. Landing in the snow-covered King's Courtyard, J'Mir rose onto his hind legs and extended his wings fully out to his sides, as Aria remained quietly perched on his back. Seconds later, King J'Amal Aidin Kondur uncloaked, appearing directly in front of them.

"Welcome, J'Mir Mahajan," said King J'Amal Aidin Kondur, rising to his hind legs and spreading his wings while standing chest-to-chest and face-to-face with the ascendant dragon king. "You have grown, my son."

"Thank you, Father," replied J'Mir Mahajan. "My wingspan may eventually grow to fill your shadow, but your legacy shall remain an eternal and irreplaceable monument to your reign as king."

Without further words, both dragons took to the sky. Within seconds, they were plunging deep into the Bay of Bengal, one hundred miles south of Calcutta. Descending to the bottom of the ocean, they headed north where they entered a narrow opening in the continental shelf of India. They followed the watery passageway for several hundred miles, traveling beneath the northeastern corner of India, through Nepal, and into a subterranean cavern at the base of the Himalaya Mountain Range. From there, they ascended through a series of interconnected watery caverns before finally breaching the surface inside a space untouched by sunlight since the dawn of time.

Upon emerging from the hidden lagoon, the scales along King J'Amal Aidin Kondur's neck began venting light, revealing an enormous chamber deep inside the granite heart of one of the many nameless peaks of the Himalayas. The gilded surfaces, painted by the blood of countless generations of dragons, reflected light from walls that extended thousands of feet upward, revealing innumerable ancient tombs carved deep into the stone to create individual burial crypts.

Mimicking the actions of his father, J'Mir Mahajan's scales also began to glow, adding his illumination to that of King J'Amal Aidin Kondur. Their combined glow revealed several large tombs carved into the walls at the lowest level of the ancestral dragon burial chamber. As their eyes traveled around the circumference, they came to rest on a freshly excavated crypt with coal and lava stone stacked neatly in a large pile near the opening.

Aria Wong slid gracefully down J'Mir Mahajan's lowered wing and waited respectfully near the water's edge as her dragon joined King J'Amal Aidin Kondur.

Standing chest to chest with their long necks partially intertwined, King J'Amal Aidin Kondur said, "J'Mir Mahajan, my blood is your blood. My strength is your strength. My wisdom is your wisdom. My destiny is your destiny. My kingdom is your kingdom."

Responding, J'Mir Mahajan said, "King J'Amal Aidin Kondur, your blood is my blood. Your strength is my strength. Your wisdom is my wisdom. Your destiny is my destiny. Your kingdom is my kingdom."

Following their exchange, J'Amal Aidin Kondur turned and approached the stack of coal and lava stone, consuming half of it before backing into the burial crypt. Striking his head against the ceiling of the crypt, the rock inside tumbled downward, closing the opening. As his final act, he expelled his fiery breath against the stones, melting them to create an airtight seal.

Outside the crypt, J'Mir Mahajan consumed the remaining carbon, using it to expel fire into the walls above King J'Amal Aidin Kondur's tomb. The superheated molten gold cascaded down the wall, sealing the crypt for all eternity. Before it cooled completely, J'Mir Mahajan beckoned Aria to come nearer. Together, they pressed their right hands against the center of the portal, permanently imprinting
it with their royal seals. Afterwards, they returned to the edge of the lagoon, where they waited in silence.

Standing there, outside the tomb of King J'Amal Aidin Kondur, J'Mir was oddly reminded of the noble elephant he had escorted to its final resting place beneath a canopy of trees during the ivory challenge. The reality of the current moment further amplified the importance of the lessons learned during the challenge in Ahl Sha H'Araah. The passing of both noble giants happened away from the prying eyes of others to preserve the dignity and respect they had rightfully earned. This time, it was his own father, and he would vigilantly protect and preserve both the legacy and the remains of this passing giant.

Within a few minutes, J'Mir and Aria could sense the slowing of King J'Amal Aidin Kondur's massive heart. A few seconds later it stopped.

There is never so much as a single heartbeat separating the rule of dragon kings. The instant of one dragon king's final exhalation occurs simultaneously with the inhalation of his ascendant's.

Solemnly, Aria climbed the lowered wing of her dragon, taking her place at the base of his neck, just in front of his wings before the two of them slipped back into the lagoon. Retracing their path through the watery caverns and subterranean aqueducts, they passed beneath Nepal and India. The dragon king ascendant who had entered the opening in the continental shelf, now emerged from it as King J'Mir Mahajan, ruler of the Northeastern Dragon Kingdom.

As he and his bonded rider slowly circled the Earth, following the border between the light of day and the dark of night, the glowing golden light of other dragons flashed beneath them, honoring the passing of one king and heralding the ascension of another. Even the King of Kings, T'Aer Bolun Dakkar and Jacob Payne, delayed their return to Nin'Jahlah and the realm of Ahl Sha H'Araah, to honor the inaugural flight of King J'Mir Mahajan and his bonded rider, Aria Wong. When they crossed back into the northeastern quadrant, the new dragon king was joined by his brothers, T'Pal and Mi'Kael Mahajan, who escorted him as his primary lieutenants across Asia to the sky above Singapore, before breaking off and returning to their own individual lairs.

Two dragons observing the inaugural flight from below did not share in the joy and reverence of the majority. In fact, they had lain in wait, intending to challenge and attack the new dragon king as he crossed the Tibetan Plateau. With T'Pal and Mi'Kael Mahajan unexpectedly joining him on the final leg of his journey, Xiana Safir and Mi'Kah D'Monicus opted to delay their deadly ambush. They had a full century of opportunities ahead of them in which to challenge and unseat him, and sooner than later, he would be alone.

The problem with planning and training in a vacuum is that the information you base your strategies on, must remain static for your plans to be effective. Running the same simulations over and over again will undoubtedly increase your effectiveness in beating the simulation; however, when confronting an opponent who has progressed through several stages of evolution while challenging themselves to constantly develop new tactics and strategies, you may as well be fighting a punching bag. When that opponent has trained with the King of Kings and his bonded rider, unless you *are* King T'Aer Bolun Dakkar and Jacob Payne is feeding you strategies and attack vectors instantaneously, your training simulations will be as useless as pounding quicksand.

While it would be impossible to absorb the thousands of battle strategies developed by Jake and T'Aer Bolun Dakkar in only a handful of years, the training they impart is as focused on mental agility as it is on physical exceptionalism. T'Aer Bolun Dakkar's ultimate objective in any battle is to incapacitate his opponent so quickly and decisively, that they can be dispatched without them suffering serious injury. In a best-case scenario, his adversary awakens with no idea what has even happened to them, and with no desire for a rematch.

King J'Mir Mahajan and Aria Wong also had another huge advantage. Neither Xiana Safir nor Mi'Kah D'Monicus were aware that the Northeastern Dragon King was bonded. For the unaware, a bonded dragon seems to have a vulnerability that an unbonded dragon does not: The missing bonding scale that protects his heart.

It would be a fool's errand for any opponent hoping to take advantage of that point of vulnerability. Although the scale is missing, the bonded rider is not, and they would literally give their lives to prevent anyone or anything from reaching it. Where the bonding scale offers passive protection, the bonded rider understands the sacrifice made by their dragon, and the faith he has placed in them to protect that voluntary vulnerability. Accordingly, the passion with which they will defend their dragon's heart cannot even be measured.

Were someone to ask a bonded rider to describe the connection to their dragon, at first, they would hear only silence, for that connection transcends the human range of emotional expression. It is a constant yearning that never wanes. Even after twenty years of forced separation, Svend Erickson's commitment to King Kai Bok Katari remained an insuppressible need that never faded or diminished in intensity. The immediate love Sibyl Dupree felt the instant she recognized King Sha'Kaa Santiago leaping towards her, immediately rendered all worldly possessions devoid of value to her. When an eleven-year-old Jake placed his hand against the face of T'Aer Bolun Dakkar in the middle of a back-country road, the entire world suddenly became a different place for him; one in which he could not live without his amazing dragon.

The rarity of Aria's Przewalski's horse was an infinitesimal distraction compared to the depth of the connection she felt to King J'Mir Mahajan, even before he stepped out of her dreams and into her reality.

Without understanding the inseverable connection dragons share with their bonded riders, it is impossible to defeat them. Once that connection *is* understood, it is senseless to even try.

Xiana Safir had spent years stoking the flames of resentment inside the mind of her offspring, Mi'Kah D'Monicus. So severely had she damaged him, that he was about to enter an arena he was entirely unprepared for, to face an opponent he was wholly incapable of defeating, all in an attempt to satisfy a six-headed Hydra dragoness, who lacked the capacity to even *feel* contentment. For both Xiana Safir and Mi'Kah D'Monicus, it was a recipe for disaster, the dimensions of which, they had dangerously underestimated.

CHAPTER 19

WITH THE UNPRECEDENTED presence of bonded riders in each of the four dragon kingdoms, T'Aer Bolun Dakkar and Jake were both amazed at the reduction in tensions around the globe. Danni enthusiastically welcomed the addition of Aria, who immediately assisted her in creating new monitoring algorithms and improving the old ones. Together, they were able to analyze data and recognize destructive trends much faster, which increased the efficiency of their work a dozen-fold.

In travelling the world with his father for most of his childhood, Svend had acquired knowledge and behavioral data regarding nearly every terrestrial animal species on the planet. Simply by monitoring changes in their breeding and behavioral patterns, he could accurately predict environmental changes long before they spiraled out of control.

Sibyl Dupree's expertise in ancient cultures and the factors which eventually led to their demise, was of paramount importance in determining the expected outcomes of human actions and involvement on a global scale. By analyzing the trajectory of past civilizations, she could identify trends and offer solutions to prevent current societies from repeating the destructive behaviors that led to the downfall of entire civilizations in the past.

Jake was an expert in crushing all the data collected, into clear and understandable presentations, and striking the emotional nerves that made the urgency of change irrefutable. Not only did he recognize the potential dangers of forced cohabitation among animal species that had never shared biosystems, but he could also foresee the microbial end-results that would produce deadly, yet preventable bacterial and viral infections. By personalizing his presentations and tailoring them to emotionally impact those he needed to be "onboard" to effect the changes, he could get immediate results while others were still deep in denial.

In Nin'Jahlah, the environment was the result of King NaDahl D'Monicus's painstaking research and attention to the ways in which all species in a closed biosphere affected that environment. His life's work was visible in the world he created for his precious hybrid dinosaur offspring. When the volumes of data received from the Drokarians was added to the equation, it was blindingly clear that every problem on Earth, could be addressed with solutions the Earth itself, provided.

Likewise, forcing poisonous tree frogs into a new ecosystem where they could be eaten by venomous snakes immune to the effects of their toxin, might result in a reptilian species capable of killing every other living being on Earth. Simply stated, ignoring science in the interest of economic growth, could result in the destruction of both, unless you happen to be a snake whose diet consists exclusively of poisonous frogs.

Although there were still a myriad of issues requiring attention, with bonded riders now representing each of the four dragon kingdoms, Jake's and T'Aer Bolun Dakkar's loads were considerably lighter. Jake and Danni were able to spend more time with Sammy and Jewel, and with their tenth birthday rapidly approaching, Jake often wondered where the time had gone.

With only two weeks of summer school break remaining, Sammy and Jewel were enjoying their final weekend in Tennessee before flying back to Hawaii to start the fifth grade. Jake and Grandpa Sam were watching Sammy and his cousins from the front porch while Danni, Sarah, and Jewel, were all at the hair salon enjoying some girl-time.

As they were playing catch in the front yard, Sammy's older cousin Robbie, overthrew the ball, which sailed over Sammy's head and came to rest inside the tree line bordering the yard. Without a second thought, Sammy dashed off after it. When he bent over to pick it up, a large timber rattler, coiled and struck him in the upper arm. Sammy dropped the ball and came running out of the woods with the rattler still dangling from his sleeve.

Jake leapt from the porch, landing in the yard almost twenty feet from the steps. He reached Sammy within seconds, yanking the snake from his arm, and flinging it nearly a hundred yards over the trees and back into the woods. Tearing open the sleeve of Sammy's shirt, he frantically searched for the snake bite. When he found it, it was already fading, with two shiny black spots quickly returning to his normal flesh tone.

Big Sam got there a few seconds later, carrying a snake bite kit.

"Where did it get him?" asked Samuel frantically.

"I think it just got caught in his shirt sleeve," said Jake. "There are no bite marks that I can find."

Carefully inspecting the area, just as Jake had done, Samuel couldn't find the bite marks either. Looking at his grandson, he asked, "Are you okay, Sammy?"

"I think so," said Sammy. "It startled me, but I didn't feel anything."

"Well, maybe we should call it a day," Jake said. We'll get you inside and keep an eye on you just in case."

"I'm fine, Dad," said Sammy. "I don't think he got me at all."

"Still," said Jake. "Let's get you inside and find another shirt for you. We can't have you running around like this when your mom gets back."

"Okay," said Sammy, obviously disappointed that their game of catch had been interrupted.

"You guys can pick up your game again tomorrow," said Jake. "It's getting late anyway, and I need you to help me toss some burgers on the grill."

"Oh Boy!" said Sammy. "Hamburgers are my favorite!"

Inside the house, Jake checked Sammy's arm again to make sure he hadn't missed anything. He noticed a safety pin on the dresser in the guestroom and picked it up saying, "Close your eyes for a second, Son. I want to try something, so tell me if you feel anything."

Opening the safety pin, he quickly poked Sammy's arm with it. As he suspected, Sammy didn't feel a thing, because his entire arm immediately deployed body armor identical to Jake's! Smiling to himself, Jake said, "Okay, son. You're fine. Go ahead and change your shirt and meet me outside so we can get the grill going."

"Incredible," said T'Aer Bolun Dakkar from beyond the veil of Ahl Sha H'Araah. "You are the first bonded rider to ever father a child after bonding with a dragon. Evidently, Sammy has inherited some of the traits that *we* share."

"Which would certainly explain why he's never been scratched, cut, or bruised before," said Jake. "Unlike Jewel, who gets the same nicks and bruises as any other ten-year-old."

"Male dragons become their fathers, and females become their mothers," said T'Aer Bolun Dakkar. "Apparently, the same holds true for our bonded riders."

"Which also explains why the pride never even comes close to hurting the twins, no matter how close they follow," said Jake. "They're being guided by Jewel. She's connected to them the very same way that Danni is."

"That would also seem to confirm my own observations while watching them," said T'Aer Bolun Dakkar.

"Well, that adds a whole new level to the 'birds and bees' conversation," said Jake. "*That* should be interesting," he added with a smile.

The dual dimensions of the Payne twins had magically coalesced for them, giving them the absolute best of both worlds. They instinctively understood the need for discretion when it came to their home in Nin'Jahlah. As far as they were concerned, they lived in Honolulu. They attended school there, and just like other children, they had homework and soccer practice and bedtimes, and Jake and Danni regularly attended PTA meetings just as the parents of other children did. It was important for Jake and Danni, that Sammy and Jewel were not isolated from society, despite the extraordinary circumstances surrounding their home life. As a result, they were well-adjusted and very well-mannered children who were the joy of Jake's and Danni's existence.

If only Mi'Kah D'Monicus had experienced that time of love and support from Xiana Safir and Bokur D'Monicus, perhaps he would not be minutes away from doing something idiotic.

All dragons can sense the proximity of related or non-related dragons through their genetically inherited tug of familiarity. On the other hand, dragon kings can delineate between family bloodlines when that tug is sensed. During his flight of ascension with King J'Amal Aidin Kondur following his selection by the Conference of Kings, J'Mir Mahajan had basically received a genetic handshake from each dragon residing in the Northeastern Dragon Kingdom. Accordingly, he could identify dragons of a specific bloodline when other dragons simply recognized a single dragon king.

King J'Mir Mahajan and Aria noticed Mi'Kah D'Monicus shadowing them from a position above and behind them. This was a tactic typically employed by Hydra dragons preceding an attack. Although Hydra dragons are deadly once they are in range of their targets, their multiple heads and necks make them far less maneuverable than other dragon species during flight. Even though Mi'Kah D'Monicus was not a Hydra dragon, that specific attack strategy clearly revealed that his battle plan was developed by his mother Xiana Safir.

Mi'Kah D'Monicus would attempt to take advantage of the blind spot common to all dragons *except* Hydras, who can maintain a full three-hundred-sixty-degree field of vision due to their multiple heads. When he saw King J'Mir Mahajan apparently focusing on and targeting a large bait ball of Indian Oceanic herring, he quickly descended to launch his attack. In order to maintain the element of surprise, Aria was literally attached to the underside of King J'Mir Mahajan's neck, peeking upward from beneath the cover of his wings.

With King J'Mir Mahajan being the larger of the two dragons, it was crucial than Mi'Kah D'Monicus strike the area just behind the dragon king's jawline, where his armor scaling transitioned to the leathery skin covering his head. If he could reach that area before King J'Mir Mahajan could react, he could bring down the dragon king in a matter of seconds; however, his strategy contained a two-letter word that doomed it to failure: "If."

When he was within striking range, Mi'Kah D'Monicus tucked in his wings to increase his dive velocity. Less than one second before reaching his target, King J'Mir Mahajan flared his massive wings, rolling onto his back in mid-air as Aria returned to her normal riding position, which was now underneath him facing downward towards Earth. Mi'Kah D'Monicus, unable to flare his wings and reduce his airspeed, flew directly into the outstretched wings of the dragon king, who quickly sealed them around his attacker before diving into the deep black waters of the Indian Ocean.

Clinging tightly to the area directly behind his gills, Aria was able to absorb the oxygen shared with her by King J'Mir Mahajan, while the cavity created by his wings surrounding Mi'Kah D'Monicus was flushed free of it. As the captive dragon struggled fiercely against the inescapable trap suffocating him, his resistance served only to accelerate the imminent loss of consciousness. Deprived of oxygen, Mi'Kah D'Monicus slept.

It was nearly a full hour later when he awoke inside the King's Courtyard. Observing him from the seventh peak of the Crown of Earth, King J'Mir Mahajan swept into the arena just as Mi'Kah D'Monicus was attempting to stand. When he lifted his head, he found himself face-to-face with the Northeastern Dragon King.

"This is where it began," said King J'Mir Mahajan. "This is also where it should have been settled," he added. "I do not wish to be at war with you, Mi'Kah D'Monicus. Such a conflict serves no purpose when there are issues of greater importance requiring our attention. I have no quarrel with you."

For a moment, Mi'Kah D'Monicus simply laid there on the floor of the arena. He was embarrassed by his effortless defeat at the hands of the king, and ashamed of his own behavior. Six years ago, they had stood side-by-side in this arena, proudly vying for the rights to the title of King. J'Mir Mahajan had earned the crown that

Mi'Kah had attempted to steal with this cowardly sneak-attack gone wrong.

"Please forgive me," said Mi'Kah D'Monicus, awkwardly rising to his feet as the fog slowly lifted from his oxygen deprived mind. "I am unworthy of your forgiveness, but I ask for your mercy as my king."

"You have broken no law, and I take no offense at your right to challenge my reign," replied the dragon king. "There will be many who will test my worthiness to rule during the coming century, and I must rise to meet those challenges, whether they are announced in advance or simply executed spontaneously. If I cannot rise to meet the unexpected, then it is I who am not worthy."

For Mi'Kah D'Monicus, it was as if losing consciousness had re-booted his sensibilities. His quarrel was not with King J'Mir Mahajan; it was with a certain Hydra dragoness who he had allowed to goad him into this baseless confrontation.

"You are truly a wise and honorable king," said Mi'Kah D'Monicus. "You shall have my respect and my loyalty from this day forward, and should you require my service to any degree, you shall have it."

"Thank you, my friend," said King J'Mir Mahajan. "Now go in peace."

Without further discussion, Mi'Kah D'Monicus took to the sky, vanishing into the darkness.

"I am proud of you," said Aria, stepping forth from the shadows of the King's Courtyard. "You have done well, King J'Mir Mahajan, and I am honored by the bond we share."

Lowering his wing for Aria to climb aboard, J'Mir Mahajan could not have been more pleased. Together, they had faced their first challenger and emerged victorious, and their bond was now stronger than ever.

As they rose into the sky and merged with the stars above, Jake and King T'Aer Bolun Dakkar watched from the seventh peak of the Crown of Earth. "Well done, my friend," said Jake, as they too took flight, disappearing into the veil of Ahl Sha H'Araah.

CHAPTER 20

FOR A MOTHER who had grown accustomed to discovering exceptional things about her children, Danni was unremarkably calm when Jake told her about Sammy's and Jewel's enhanced abilities. Apparently, living in an alternative dimension with four hundred hybrid dinosaurs and a dragon king, had somewhat dampened her reaction to news that would have floored anyone else.

"So, our son is indestructible, and our daughter speaks to dinosaurs," said Danni with a smile. "Why does that not surprise me?" she asked rhetorically.

"Possibly because our friends ride dragons and we use alien technology to solve the world's environmental problems," said Jake somewhat casually. Looking at her, he added, "Or, because you are an amazing mother and it's only natural that your kids are extraordinary too."

"I'm gonna go with all of the above," said Danni, smiling at him. "I've also discovered something amazing and unusual. It took me a while to figure it out, but after testing my hypotheses I was able to solve the mystery," she added.

"And what might that mystery be?" asked Jake curiously.

"When was the last time you or I, or either of the kids were ill? You know; a common cold, the flu, bronchitis, measles, chickenpox, shingles, or anything for that matter?"

"I haven't even had the sniffles since I was nine or ten," said Jake. "Come to think of it, I can't remember either of the kids ever being sick," he added.

"Exactly," said Danni. "And I haven't had so much as a fever in over a decade. With you and Turbo jet-setting around the globe on a daily basis, it would've been impossible for you not to have been exposed to any number of viruses and bacteria. They would have invariably affected either you, me, or the kids, yet none of us have been sick for years."

"I'm guessing it's not because of our ironclad immunities," said Jake.

"That could play a limited role," said Danni. "But there had to have been something else; another factor that boosted our chances over those of constantly-evolving bacteria and viruses. Then I remembered our trip to Bogota to meet Mr. Torres."

"We've been to Columbia a number of times before and since then," said Jake.

"Yes," said Danni. "But that was the first time I had ever been to Ahl Sha H'Araah. I distinctly remember having felt the flu coming on. You know; the sluggishness, mild fever, and body aches that tell you the rest of your week is about to turn to crap."

"Yes," said Jake. "But I don't recall you being sick, either before or after our trip."

"Right again," said Danni. "Because bacteria and viruses cannot survive inside the interdimensional rift. Just passing through it into Ahl Sha H'Araah, instantly kills them, rendering them inert. At first, I thought it was something here in Nin'Jahlah, but actually, the bacteria and viruses here cannot survive crossing Ahl Sha H'Araah either."

"So, it's like a decontamination chamber between dimensions," said Jake.

"Precisely!" exclaimed Danni. "It effectively kills any virus or bacteria that passes through it without affecting the host or the enzymes that support the host's biological functions."

"That is so amazing!" exclaimed Jake. "Ahl Sha H'Araah is what prevents viruses and bacteria from passing between dimensions, so we could theoretically kill them by bringing them here."

"Not just in theory, Jake! It works every single time!" said Danni excitedly. "Picture the interdimensional rift, or trans-dimensional rift, or Ahl Sha H'Araah, or whatever you want to call it, as a decontamination chamber that must be crossed in order to pass out of, or into any other dimension. It strips away viruses and bacteria instantly without regard to where they originate, or the bio-organism to which they are attached."

Amazed, Jake said, "That means, if we could expose infected patients to Ahl Sha H'Araah for as little as one second,"

"We can cure them instantly!" interrupted Danni. "I've tested it on dozens of different bacteria and virus strains, and the results were consistent and instantaneous. It even kills the Drokarian Livia bacterium. Best of all, the inert virus still causes the development of antibodies that trigger the body's own immune defenses to prevent reinfection."

"That is amazing!" exclaimed Jake. "If we can find a way to expose infected individuals to the healing effects of Ahl Sha H'Araah, we could revolutionize the pharmaceutical industry."

"Indeed, we could," Danni agreed. "Aria and I have been working on a design similar to an MRI scanner that would allow controlled exposure by passing patients through a containment tube from head-to-toe. Inside the tube would be an ultra-thin veil through which they'd pass, never even realizing they had traveled through a dimensional portal. When they emerged from the scanner, they would be completely free of all bacterial and viral infections. The treatment would take only a few seconds as opposed to weeks of antibiotics and antiviral medications."

"And how close are you to having a working prototype?" asked Jake.

"The scanning tube is already complete," said Danni. "We were able to produce all of the parts using the three-dimensional printer in our Honolulu office, but Aria is still working on the physics of creating a standardized and stable dimensional mini-portal. In theory it must be possible, but we haven't quite figured that part out yet."

"Yeah, and staffing hospitals and clinics with dragons and hybrid dinosaurs is out of the question," said Jake, jokingly.

"True, but there must be a way to analyze their brainwaves and synapse responses when they open portals into Ahl Sha H'Araah," replied Danni. "If we can identify and isolate those electronic or electromagnetic frequencies triggered when they open a portal, we might be able to synthesize them and recreate the results in a laboratory under controlled conditions."

"It would certainly be worth a shot," agreed Jake. "But we need to be exceedingly careful in how we reveal this technology. Letting it fall into the hands of the wrong people could quickly turn the dream into a nightmare, so let's proceed with the utmost of caution."

"Of course," said Danni. "Aria doesn't document or write anything down outside our office in Hawaii, and like you, she does most of the math in her head, so there won't be a paper trail. I keep all of the compiled data and device schematics here in Nin'Jahlah, so other than the three of us, no one even knows we're working on it."

"As always, you're way ahead of the game," said Jake. "I just want to make sure we have all of the patents and copyrights in place, and a functional device to roll out before anyone even sees it coming. The pharmaceutical companies are going to blow a gasket when they find out we can cure all bacterial and viral infections instantly, without using any of their meds."

"That's putting it mildly," said Danni. "If we can work out the details of the mini-portal technology, countries will be able to eliminate viral pandemics and epidemics nearly as soon as they appear, saving millions of lives."

"And costing the pharmaceutical companies billions of dollars in lost revenue," added Jake. "The last thing we need is another billion-dollar contract on our heads."

"I'm not a big fan of those," said Danni. "But this will undoubtedly change worldwide healthcare as we know it. Hospitals will be able to stop the spread of bacterial and viral infections, and literally cure their patients with a 3-D printer."

"The world is going to love you, but big pharma is going to do everything possible to discredit you, and vilify the procedure," said Jake.

"It wasn't that long ago when scarificators and leaches were considered the height of modern medicine, and lobotomies were heralded as an effective treatment for schizophrenia," said Danni. "Currently, it takes up to four years to develop a vaccine for a novel virus, and during that time, hundreds of thousands of people die, waiting for a cure that never comes, or comes too late."

Taking Jake's hands and looking into his eyes, she said, "Jake, what if Sammy or Jewel were the ones infected, and all we could do was sit helplessly by, praying for a cure? This is that cure, Jake. We pass through it every day, and we are living proof that it's safe and effective. For every Sammy and Jewel out there waiting for an answer to their prayers, this could change everything, and I'm willing to fight for it no matter who it upsets!"

Jake had to smile despite the seriousness of their discussion. It was largely due to her passion for life that formerly uninhabitable regions of the planet had recovered and were thriving again. She was willing to fight for the lives of every living thing on Earth, and if the pharmaceutical companies were going to butt heads with her on this, they'd better be wearing helmets.

"You're doing it again," said Jake.

"Doing what again?" asked Danni, slightly distracted by his observation.

"Everything perfectly," answered Jake with a smile. "And if it's a fight they're looking for, we'll deliver it right to their doorsteps." Taking her face in his hands, he kissed her before saying, "If there's a way to replicate the portal, we will find it together. It wouldn't be the first impossible thing we've accomplished."

Smiling at him, she asked, "Have you any idea how much I love you, Mr. Payne?"

"As a matter of fact, Mrs. Payne, I think I've just about got it narrowed down enough to make an educated guess," said Jake.

They were still smiling when Jewel walked into the room with one of the giant chocolate chip cookies Sarah baked for them while they were in Tennessee.

"Where did you get that?" asked Danni, curiously.

"Grandma Sarah baked it for us," said Jewel.

"I mean, how did you get it here?" asked Danni, amazed she could have somehow stashed it in her backpack before they left Tennessee.

"They were in the cookie jar next to the oven," said Jewel. "I brought one for Sammy. Did you want one too?"

"What do you mean, you brought one for Sammy," asked Jake, totally confused at the bizarre turn the conversation had taken.

"I went to Grandma and Grandpa Payne's house," said Jewel, biting into the giant cookie.

"When did you go to Grandma's and Grandpa's house?" asked Danni, her eyes wide with wonder.

"Just now," said Jewel as Sammy walked in with another half-eaten cookie. "She said I could visit any time I wanted to," Jewel added.

"And you just popped in tonight for a cookie?" asked Jake. "What did Grandma say when she saw you?"

"She didn't see me," said Jewel. "She and Grandpa were already sleeping so I didn't wake them up."

"How did you get there, Sweetheart?" asked Jake.

"Tikka showed me how to open the window," said Jewel before asking, "Are you sure you don't want one?"

CHAPTER 21

FROM THE MOUTHS OF BABES emerge the most shocking of things. As Jewel and Sammy stood there with chocolate adorning the corners of their mouths, Jake and Danni were speechless. The casual manner in which Jewel revealed that she could open a portal through Ahl Sha H'Araah, and the ease with which she pinpointed her exit location on the other side of it, was truly extraordinary. There are multiple billions of alternate dimensions accessible through the trans-dimensional rift. Had Tikka not guided T'Aer Bolun Dakkar to Nin'Jahlah, even he would never have found it.

"Jewel honey, how long have you known how to open the window to Grandma's and Grandpa's house," asked Danni, trying her hardest to remain calm and clear-headed.

"Since we came back a week ago," answered Jewel. "Sammy said he wished he had one of Grandma's cookies, and then I wanted one too!" Feeling the need to further explain, she added, "Grandma said that we could have one a day, and we never ate more than that."

"Sammy, do you know how to open the window too?" asked Jake, curiously.

"Uh-uh," said Sammy. "I can't hear Tikka like Jewel can," he mumbled, trying to speak around a mouth full of cookie.

"Jewel, how did you know which window to open?" asked Danni.

"Tikka only showed me one window," said Jewel. "That was the window to Grandma and Grandpa. Tikka's not gonna get in trouble, is she?" asked Jewel, suddenly afraid she'd said too much.

"Heavens no!" said Danni. "Actually, I think Tikka may have just given us an answer we've been searching for. We just need to figure out how she did it."

"I'm sure she can tell you," said Jewel. "Going to Grandma's house was really easy!"

"You know, sweetheart," said Danni. "That's exactly what I'll do. But first, it's time for you and Sammy to finish your cookies and get ready for bed, Okay?"

"Okay, Mom," said Jewel, finishing her cookie and heading down the hallway with Sammy to their bedrooms.

"One more thing," said Danni before they entered their rooms. "No more trips to visit Grandma and Grandpa without permission from me or your dad, Okay?"

"Yes, Ma'am," said Jewel and Sammy in unison before disappearing into their rooms.

"I never would have seen that coming," said Jake. "All you need to do is ask Tikka, and…"

"I just did," interrupted Danni with a sly smile. "And now, I know how she does it."

Tikka and Danni had been able to transfer enormous clusters of information since the day they bonded. In order to make sense of it, the questions needed to be extremely specific; otherwise, it was like starting an avalanche by poking the mountain with a stick. Jewel's questions were posed with the specificity of a laser pointer. She had asked Tikka how to get to Grandma's kitchen, and Tikka gave her the specific answer to the question she'd been asked. Danni's question for Tikka was a bit broader, and the truckload of data she'd received in response contained answers to every possible follow-up question she could have asked.

King NaDahl D'Monicus had spent centuries mapping the portals of Ahl Sha H'Araah. The grid system he devised was as precise as it was extensive, and since it was a part of the permanent memory, he shared with his female dinosaur mates, it had been genetically passed on to his offspring. It was remarkably similar to the geographic coordinate system used by humans, but it didn't use imaginary lines superimposed onto an image of the globe. It used the specific threads of Earth's magnetic field to identify relative positions on the planet's surface as they corresponded to their counter locations in the different dimensions accessible through Ahl Sha H'Araah. Although it would have taken a million dragon lifetimes to map the infinite number of portal locations in parallel dimensions accessible from Earth, the exit and reentry points on Earth were complete and accurate to within approximately one meter and they numbered in the trillions!

These portals were activated using the infrasonic frequencies with which dragons emitted their tug of familiarity; the same frequencies that Jake had identified and suppressed during the Drokarian dragon harvest crisis. By targeting the specified point on Earth's magnetic field grid with that ultra-low frequency, it caused a temporary disruption in the veil of Ahl Sha H'Araah, creating the window Jewel had spoken of.

Since Tikka had only given Jewel one set of exit and reentry coordinates, the only route she could possibly travel was from their front porch in Nin'Jahlah, to Grandma Payne's kitchen in Tennessee, and back again. While it was still unclear how Jewel managed to produce the correct subsonic frequency, her attempts to traverse Ahl Sha H'Araah in both directions had undeniably been successful.

Although dragons routinely crossed into Ahl Sha H'Araah, other than T'Aer Bolun Dakkar, most of them remained there in order to run training scenarios or to project their visual avatars from one side of it while remaining concealed on the other. At the conclusion of their purpose there, they would return to the dimension from which they had come. King T'Aer Bolun Dakkar was the only dragon who routinely crossed the void of Ahl Sha H'Araah into other dimensions, but the technique used by dragons was vastly different than the exacting system developed by King NaDahl D'Monicus. Since dragons instinctively knew where they were because of their genetically inherited mapping system, NaDahl D'Monicus had obviously created this magnetic grid chart in the event either his dragon or dinosaur offspring needed a detailed map of the dimensions beyond the veil of Ahl Sha H'Araah.

Regardless of the reasoning behind it, this was an intricately detailed diagram that could be adapted for use in developing the mini portal system. It was the breakthrough that Danni and Aria had been hoping for, and now, thanks to the Jewel of Nin'Jahlah, it was well within reach.

With Tikka's help, it took fewer than twenty days to create a mapping system that covered Earth's inhabited land masses. By using the physical locations of specialty clinics and hospitals around the globe, the scanning tube, dubbed the Magnetic Resonance Chamber (MRC), could be assembled onsite and precisely aligned using the portal grid system created by King NaDahl D'Monicus. The subsonic frequency would target two adjacent grid coordinates along the Earth's magnetic field as the exit and reentry points through Ahl Sha H'Araah, opening a window of exactly one square meter.

Within a month, efficacy trials were already being conducted on volunteers in twenty different countries, with critically ill patients receiving priority. Prior to treatment, the procedure was explained, and questions were answered, which actually took longer than the treatment itself. After covering their eyes with solarium goggles, patients would glide along rails through the MRC, secured to a bed outfitted with rubber rollers. It took between five and seven seconds for a patient's entire body to pass into and out of Ahl Sha H'Araah, at a speed of one foot per second, after which, they were free of all live bacterial and viral infections.

Following the treatment, patients were overjoyed at the immediate cessation of symptoms, and within hours, their conditions had markedly improved. Even patients who had been critically ill, were often well enough to be discharged the following day.

In order to guard against misuse of the technology, the grid coordinates were encoded, using randomly generated alphanumeric sequences that were deciphered by the proprietary software built into the MRC upon activation of the device. Once the procedure was complete, the coordinates were re-encoded and deleted from the system, so that even if the deleted coordinates were retrieved surreptitiously, they were impossible to decipher.

Rather than submitting the entire device for patent protection, each individual component of the MRC was patented separately, making it impossible to replicate the entire machine by simply switching out enough of the components to skirt the patent protections. The heart of the MRC was the magnetic sonar array, a series of powerful magnets along the inner lining of the tube. When activated, it created an invisible field which was then targeted by the subsonic frequency pulse, disrupting the veil, and opening a pathway through Ahl Sha H'Araah.

The device hit the medical and pharmaceutical industries like a thermonuclear blast; however, since most of the components could be produced locally and assembled within one day, it was impossible to interrupt supply chains, disrupt production, or otherwise interfere with the deployment of the devices. They could be made nearly anywhere, by nearly anyone with access to a 3-D printer, using four-foot by eight-foot panels of plastic, plexiglass, or fiberglass. The industrial magnets and commercial sonar devices were also readily available from numerous suppliers around the world. While it was preferred that the devices be used inside medical facilities, they were just as effective even if they were used in an automotive garage, industrial warehouse, or a shopping mall massage studio.

The heart of the system was the magnetic field grid targeting software developed by Jake, Danni, and Aria, and without that, it was impossible to open the pathway through Ahl Sha H'Araah. While the actual targeting grid data never left the seclusion of Nin'Jahlah, Jake and Danni were happy to provide the individualized targeting codes for the devices to anyone able to prove their benevolent intent.

The income generated by the patents was divided into thirds, with two-thirds going to Payne International, and the remaining third going to the newly founded corporation, Aria Wong Singapore (AWS). With her first official business enterprise, Aria's financial independence had been secured far into the future.

When the news of Aria's billion-dollar startup hit the web, it sent financial ripples across the entire Asian theater. Within a few months, AWS was one of Singapore's largest employers, nearly rivalling her father's business, WEI-Singapore. Although she was in constant contact with Jake and Danni, who maintained the grid coordinate codes in Nin'Jahlah for security reasons, Aria ran her company remotely from her grandfather's farm. Despite her company's success, she preferred the peace and tranquility of Kranji Countryside to the bright lights and fast pace of Singapore City. There, she could spend nearly every moment of her free time with her treasured Przewalski's horse, J'Mir.

Late one Friday evening after finishing up the code assignments needed for her clients in Vietnam the following day, her personal assistant in the Singapore head office put through a call for her. It was Leung Fu. He wanted to schedule a meeting.

CHAPTER 22

ARIA WAS MORE THAN HAPPY to schedule an appointment with Mr. Fu. Despite his somewhat shady business tactics, he was also one of Hong Kong's most influential proprietors of legitimate businesses in Mainland China and throughout Southeast Asia.

With infectious diseases claiming the lives of nearly twenty million people each year, most of them could be prevented with a seven second trip through the MRC. Now that the procedure had been approved for use by the United States Food and Drug Administration, the Center for Disease Control, the European Medicines Agency, and the World Health Organization, sales and production of the devices were skyrocketing.

The impact on international stock markets was shocking and immediate. Payne International held patents and copyrights on some of the world's most innovative technologies and whenever they were involved, markets responded positively and enthusiastically. This new medical apparatus was so effective, it created a seismic shift in the way infections were treated, curing patients without subjecting them to the side effects of prescription medications, a substantial source of Leung Fu's business income.

"I have a 5:00 p.m. appointment available on Wednesday," said Aria. "I'd be happy to set it aside for you."

"I would prefer an earlier date," said Leung Fu. "I will be in Singapore tomorrow morning."

"Unfortunately, Wednesday evening is the earliest I can meet with you," Aria replied. "I will be traveling over the weekend and will not return until Tuesday afternoon."

"Perhaps you should consider re-scheduling your trip," said Mr. Fu. "I am a very, very busy man, and I do not like to be kept waiting."

"In Vietnam, there is a rural clinic near Ho Chi Minh City, battling a multi-resistant intestinal bacterial infection that is claiming the lives of children," Aria replied. "The MRCs are being assembled as we speak, and I will be traveling there with my team to supervise the installation and initial treatments. Afterwards, we will provide training for the laboratory technicians and medical personnel who will be administering the procedures. Their patients have been waiting much longer than the five days between now and my proposed appointment time with you. I'm sure you can understand the urgency of their situation."

"What I understand, is that while you are stomping around in the mud tending to Vietnamese peasants, something dreadful could happen to your grandfather in Kranji Countryside," said Mr. Fu in a voice thick with indignation.

"Your concern for my family is quite touching, Mr. Fu," said Aria. "Perhaps we can add it to our list of discussion topics for Wednesday at 5:00 p.m." After five seconds of silence on the other end of the call, Aria said, "Have a nice weekend, Mr. Fu, and I will see you at my office in Singapore City on Wednesday."

Without another word, Aria ended the call, continuing her trip preparations with barely a second thought. The security systems and protocols at AWS's main office in Singapore City were even more advanced than those of her father's company, and here in Kranji Countryside, her grandfather could not have been safer.

In the pasture behind the barn, an unusual meeting was occurring between a Przewalski's horse and a snow leopard. After only a few minutes, the snow leopard paced off into the dense jungle surrounding the farm, and the horse that had been basking in the sun-soaked pasture the entire day, resumed grazing peacefully.

King J'Mir Mahajan and Aria Wong arrived in Ho Chi Minh City early Saturday morning. Their advance team had already assembled the MRCs inside medical tents provided by the World Health Organization, and there were long lines wrapped around each of them. After entering the activation codes containing the encrypted portal coordinates, Aria and her team began processing patients through the MRCs. During the first hour, they processed a total of seventy patients through the three tents. During the second hour, that number had increased to nearly four hundred, and by the end of the day, approximately five thousand patients had been cured of the infection. Two additional MRCs had also been printed and assembled, and the activation codes for them had already been purchased.

Later that evening, Aria called to check on her grandfather, who answered the phone quite excitedly, saying, "Aria, you will not believe what I saw today!"

"What was it, Opa?" asked Aria, curiously.

"A snow leopard!" replied Shen. "It was near the edge of the jungle in the pasture behind the barn!"

"Are the farm animals and J'Mir okay?" asked Aria, already aware that King J'Mir Mahajan's holograph would follow the predefined path he'd taken through the pasture on the previous day.

"The animals are fine," said Shen. "They are already in the barn for the evening, and the snow leopard is just casually patrolling the edge of the jungle."

"Did you call anyone to come and check it out?" asked Aria.

"Of course not!" exclaimed Shen. "I have a Przewalski's horse *and* an endangered snow leopard on *my* farm! That is undoubtedly a positive sign from heaven, and I will not allow anyone to disturb them!"

Aria was smiling broadly at Shen's excitement. "Well, I am happy for you Grandfather," she said. "I just called to make sure everything is fine and that you are well."

"Everything here is as peaceful as always, and according to the news reports, your team is doing an amazing job!" Shen replied.

"What?" asked Aria, stunned.

"You and your team are all over the news here in Singapore!" said Shen, enthusiastically. "You just keep healing people, and don't worry about me. I can take care of myself, and I will see you when you return on Tuesday."

"Okay, Opa," said Aria. "I love you. Goodnight."

"Goodnight, Granddaughter," replied Shen. "I love you too."

Outside, the sun had set, and King J'Mir Mahajan's holograph was "at rest" inside the barn. Mi'Kah D'Monicus's eyes pierced the darkness of a moonless night as they followed a black SUV slowly approaching the farmhouse with its headlights switched off. Darting into the jungle, he caught up to the slow-moving vehicle, silently shadowing it until it stopped two hundred meters from the house. Four men exited the vehicle wearing black unmarked uniforms and carrying automatic weapons with silencers attached. One of them was also carrying a cannister of kerosene.

As they approached the farm on foot, midway down the lane all of them stopped in their tracks. The large snow leopard sitting in front of them apparently had an issue with them continuing down the driveway.

"Shoo!" whispered one of the men loudly while gesturing for the big cat to move out of the way.

Instead, the snow leopard lowered its body and began the characteristic side-to-side wiggling motion that conveyed an unmistakable message: "You are about to become my dinner!"

Before the men could even raise their weapons, the snow leopard charged, pouncing on the squad leader at the head of the group, driving him forcefully into the ground. The rest of the men, holding their fire to avoid shooting their colleague, panicked, and scattered, seeking cover in the jungle lining both sides of the lane.

Mi'Kah D'Monicus moved through the dense underbrush like a deadly shadow. The men were trembling with fear as they watched the dark driveway, hoping to catch a glimpse of the snow leopard and get a clean shot at it. As they hid like children caught up in a terrifying life or death game of hide and seek, Mi'Kah D'Monicus systematically picked them off one by one, removing their weapons and dragging their unconscious bodies back to the center of the lane.

When they awoke and slowly sat up, the snow leopard was still there; however, their weapons were not. Without a sound, the men began scooting along the ground back down the lane. After creating some separation between themselves and the deadly predator stalking them, they scrambled to their feet and ran for their lives back to the SUV. Upon reaching it, they all piled in frantically, anxious to get away from there as quickly as possible. When he started the vehicle and switched on the headlights, the driver's face went completely blank.

On the hood of the SUV, was the kerosene cannister he had been carrying. Beyond it, in the center of the access road, the snow leopard's golden eyes were brightly illuminated, and for an instant, the passengers inside the vehicle could have sworn they'd seen a dragon. Slamming the vehicle into reverse, the terrified driver backed drunkenly down the road. Finally turning around on the shoulder, he floored the gas pedal, vacating the area to the sound of screeching tires and flying gravel. Miraculously, the kerosene cannister remained affixed to the hood, all the way back to Singapore City.

Mi'Kah D'Monicus observed them from above until they dropped off the vehicle at the rental car agency and took a taxi to Jewel Changi Airport.

A few minutes later, he resumed his vigilant observation of Shen Wong's farm in Kranji Countryside, while Shen, his farm animals, and the holograph of King J'Mir Mahajan slept peacefully through the night.

The next morning, all was well on Shen's farm. The silent skirmish on the driveway leading up to the farmhouse had gone completely unnoticed, and it would be days before the cache of automatic weapons stashed in the jungle would be discovered.

At the rental car agency, the attendant noticed the kerosene cannister on the hood of the black SUV he had rented out the day before. When he walked outside and tried to remove it, he was shocked to discover it was still filled with kerosene and had literally been welded to the vehicle.

CHAPTER 23

BY THE TIME ARIA and her team left Ho Chi Minh City, they had trained several dozen nurses and laboratory technicians on the operating procedures for the MRCs and cured over fifteen thousand infected patients. She and King J'Mir Mahajan arrived in Kranji Countryside shortly before sunrise on Tuesday morning. As J'Mir returned to the barn to replace his sleeping holograph, Aria crept quietly into the house to make coffee and prepare breakfast for her grandfather.

It didn't take long for the aroma of freshly brewed coffee and scrambled eggs to lure him into the kitchen. "Good morning, Aria," said Shen, happy to see her. Hugging her, he said, "Why didn't you call? I would have been happy to pick you up at the airport."

"I know, Opa," said Aria. "I arrived earlier than expected, and I knew you would still be sleeping, so I decided to come straight here and surprise you with breakfast."

"You are such a thoughtful young woman and a wonderful granddaughter," said Shen. "It is nice to have you back at home again."

"How was your weekend," asked Aria. "Anything exciting?"

Speaking very softly, Shen said, "Come. Look over there, behind the barn."

Aria approached and stood by her grandfather. In the pasture behind the barn, the Przewalski's horse and the snow leopard were calmly standing across from each other in the dim yellow light of the rising sun. A moment later, the snow leopard turned and sauntered back into the jungle, and the horse began grazing the lush green grass blanketing the pasture.

"Aren't they amazing?" asked Shen as he stared out the kitchen window.

"They are beautiful," Aria replied. "But no more beautiful than this peaceful sanctuary you've created that attracts them."

In Hong Kong, Leung Fu was toiling over the absolute mess he had created in trying to gain leverage over Aria Wong. He'd been played like a board game, and he knew it. Whether or not Aria Wong was aware of the failed kidnapping and arson attempt, she had dictated to him the terms of their meeting and if he didn't show up, he would look like a coward. If he did show up, it would appear to others that he had been outmaneuvered by a twenty-year-old.

This was the second time his efforts at manipulating Aria Wong had ended in outright disaster. In his former years, he would have flown to Singapore himself and secured her cooperation using nothing other than his bare hands. Being manhandled by Jacob Payne inside his own office was one thing. No one other than the two of them even knew about what had occurred there. On the other hand, this incident had quickly grown legs, and knowledge of his infamous assassin squad's ineptitude had already reached the leaders of other rival triads.

For many, this would have been an opportunity for enlightenment. Perhaps the situation could be transformed into a legitimately benevolent cause. With the massive reach of his financial empire, Mr. Fu could purchase the schematics and have MRCs printed and distributed all across Asia. Except for instances when expedience was a priority, Aria had no interest in becoming a manufacturing or distribution company. By allowing third-party entrepreneurs to purchase, print, and assemble the MRCs, her company created much-needed jobs in impoverished countries as well as in thriving industrial nations. Payne International and AWS financed their corporate operations through sales of the software required to activate the portal locations where the MRCs were placed. The programming was so specific that it could only be utilized at the location where an MRC had been installed and meticulously aligned. Once it was moved by more than ten centimeters in any direction, it would require new portal codes.

The opportunities for enterprising companies and ambitious entrepreneurs were astonishing. A company that purchased the 3-D printer software, could produce an unlimited number of MRCs, each of which were issued a unique, non-sequential serial number. If the serial numbers were incorrect, the portal software would not work, preventing even the most skilled hackers from cracking or bypassing the encryption protocols. With a nominal investment, companies could literally begin production and distribution of the MRCs overnight.

Considering the reach of the Fu Triad, their earning potential was unlimited. By marketing and distributing a product this new and this revolutionary, they could sell millions of units all over Asia, while also earning a respectable commission on the portal activation software. Since it was impossible to flood the market with functional knockoffs, a sharp-minded individual would immediately recognize the fact that they were sitting on a veritable goldmine.

Unfortunately, Leung Fu was not a sharp-minded individual. The superiority of the Fu Triad had been achieved through gratuitous violence, merciless extortion, and a ruthless iron fist. Compromise and capitulation were two words that had been stricken from his vocabulary, as both were considered graduating stages of weakness. His corporate strategies and negotiation tactics were intentionally skewed to coerce compliance from his business partners, and in AWS, Leung Fu saw a young woman at the helm of a juggernaut, and he wanted to control all of it.

After summoning the last living member of the team who had botched the assault on Shen Wong's farm three nights earlier, Leung Fu remained locked in his vault of an office with him for several hours. When the squad leader emerged, the look of naked determination on his face was terrifying to anyone who encountered him on his trip from the 108th floor, down to the parking garage. The only reason he was still alive was because he had been the first person taken out by the snow leopard. Rather than completing their assigned mission, the others had scattered like frightened children and disappeared into the jungle. It was a mistake that his new team would most certainly not make.

Shortly before close of business at AWS, Aria's personal assistant received the call confirming her meeting with Leung Fu the following evening. Aria was legitimately excited. She hoped she could present Mr. Fu with a convincing argument and business model that would convince him to work with her as a partner in servicing Asian demand for the MRCs. With Jake's and Danni's help, they had created a presentation that, if viewed, could remove even the smallest of doubts and silence even the most boisterous of critics.

Later that evening, after Shen Wong had retired to his bedroom, King J'Mir Mahajan and Aria launched into the humid night sky above Singapore.

"You cannot trust him," said the concerned dragon. "Anyone willing to send a team of assassins to kidnap your grandfather and set fire to his farm, would not hesitate for one moment when it comes to harming you."

"I understand that he will attempt to shape the negotiations in his favor, using any means possible," answered Aria. "However, what happens after that?"

"What do you mean?" asked King J'Mir Mahajan.

"After he fails, what happens next?" repeated Aria. "He will attempt to coerce me, by using someone or something as leverage. Mathematically and logically, that makes sense. He has already failed twice, and it will obviously be an enormous embarrassment when he fails again; however, we still need a distributor in Hong Kong, and despite his arrogance and bruised ego, he has financial and logistical networks that are already in place. If we can convince him to work with us aboveboard, we can help hundreds of thousands of patients get the treatment they need almost immediately, without having to create a brand-new distribution network ourselves."

"True," said King J'Mir Mahajan. "What are the odds of us accomplishing that?"

"Approximately twenty-eight point seven to one, in our favor," replied Aria.

"Approximately?" asked King J'Mir Mahajan.

"Well, I dropped the last ten decimal places, but yes," replied Aria quite seriously. "He has far more to gain by working with us than against us, and once the bluster has been drained from his ego, he will need an 'out' that allows him to return to Hong Kong with dignity."

"Have you always been this clever?" asked the impressed dragon king.

"Clever, yes," said Aria. "Brave enough to follow through with it; well, that was all you!" she added with a smile.

A few minutes later, they were landing in the Line Island chain at the roost of King T'Aer Bolun Dakkar. After extending their wings in a formal display of acknowledgement and mutual respect, Jake and Aria dismounted to confer with one another while King J'Mir Mahajan and King of Kings T'Aer Bolun Dakkar discussed contingency plans. Despite their anticipation of major trouble in stitching this impossible deal together, Leung Fu was an extremely dangerous man, and it would be foolish to underestimate him, or the lengths to which he would go to gain a tactical advantage.

While Jake and Aria considered the most efficient means of utilizing Leung Fu's distribution network to reach as many needy patients as possible, T'Aer Bolun Dakkar and J'Mir Mahajan discussed overlapping security measures that would guarantee the safety of Aria, her family, and the employees at AWS. Once the potential points of vulnerability had been identified, and the varying levels of force that could be brought to bear were assessed, the two dragon kings felt confident they could frustrate any attempts to harm Arias loved ones, and with a plan in place, two dragon kings and two brilliant bonded riders once again ascended, merging with the stars overhead.

CHAPTER 24

LEUNG FU WAS DONE pretending to be civilized. In his mind, power unwielded was power relinquished, and he was unwilling to give another inch. His plan was to strike at so many different fronts, applying such unbearable pressure at each of them, that Aria would be unable to endure the strain and submit to his demands, no matter how excessive they may have been.

This was no longer a question of winning in a war of wills; it was about restoring the full terror his rivals felt at the mere mention of his name. It was also a matter of breaking the backs of anyone who attempted to minimize his station in Hong Kong. The Fu family name was at stake. Their legacy was on the line, and whether it was the youngest child or the oldest woman in Asia, all must tremble at the mere mention of Leung Fu. He would use Aria and her entire family as examples for anyone who would dare to question him or defy his orders.

First, he would isolate her from all her corporate allies and family members, beginning with an assault on her father's company WEI-Singapore. Next, instead of a covert four-man abduction team, he would roll through Kranji Countryside with a veritable army in broad daylight. A mountain of cash would ensure an exceptionally long response time by the Singapore Police Force, and when they did respond, Shen Wong and Leung Fu's men would already be long gone.

Leung Fu's men would sweep through Aria's family like a new broom, accounting for everyone including the WEI-Singapore regional office in Taiwan run by her siblings, Steven, and Cindy Wong. Simultaneously, his men would raid the residential compound where the rest of Aria's family lived, squashing their protective security team with overwhelming force.

The all-out assault on the WEI-Singapore and AWS enterprises would be carried out with precision timing. It was perfectly coordinated with the abduction of Sammy and Jewel Payne from the after-school activity center where they went to play and socialize with other children until Jake or Danni picked them up after work.

It is not without reason that life erects speed bumps and barriers when one is travelling a questionable path. There are a series of warning signs that could either be heeded or ignored were someone paying attention. The presentation Aria had forwarded to his office, Leung Fu had never even watched. The warning Jacob Payne had delivered directly to him inside his veritable bunker of an office, had been forgotten much too quickly. The professional assassin squad he had sent to abduct her grandfather, did not even make it beyond the driveway at Shen Wong's farm. The amount of money he was spending to conduct this global pressure campaign, far exceeded the sum of the investment required to gain exclusive regional distribution rights for the MRCs, which could be worth billions of dollars. All of these things were flashing warning signs Leung Fu had simply blown past, unable to see beyond the rage burning inside his chest, consuming his very soul.

Leung Fu's private jet landed in Singapore at 10:00 a.m. and fifteen minutes later, he was in the Presidential Suite at Marina Bay Sands. Since early that morning, he had spent most of the day with a cell phone glued to his ear, preparing for a chess game of epic proportions. His uncompromising goal was to utterly crush anyone standing between him and absolute control over the new technology that had caused his pharmaceutical stocks to plummet. By the end of the day, the entirety of Asia would remember why the Fu Triad was both respected and feared, and the insolent twenty-something CEO of AWS would be cringing in a corner, begging for mercy, and agreeing to grant any wish uttered by the powerful Leung Fu.

Assault teams and assassin squads were already staged and had been surveilling every member of Aria's immediate family since sunrise. Sammy and Jewel had been under observation since entering the on-campus after-school activity center hosted by their school in Honolulu. Danni normally arrived to pick them up, promptly at 6:30 p.m. local time, where they would be patiently waiting at the curbside pickup zone.

Shortly after Aria's departure from the farmhouse in Kranji Countryside, Leung Fu's extraction team moved in, prepared to surround and seal off the entire area. Undercover agents mingled with the tourists there visiting the farmers markets and petting zoos, keeping Shen Wong's movements under constant scrutiny. By 11:00 a.m. in Singapore, Leung Fu had received final readiness confirmations from every team leader spearheading the different facets of the operation. Those would be their final conversations until he was inside Aria's office. With everyone in place and the trap set, he felt confident enough to have a pre-celebratory lunch in the hotel's *Justin Flavours of Asia* restaurant, overlooking Marina Bay. His suite was only a ten-minute ride from AWS, so he would pull the trigger on his well-scripted mini war at noon. That would give Aria Wong plenty of time to lose her mind before he floated into her office flanked by a team of lawyers and bankers, two hours early!

Shortly before noon, after finishing his Fine Apple Tart à la mode, Leung Fu ordered the check, and pushed the "send" button on his mobile phone, transmitting the group text he been anxious to deliver all morning long: GO!

Everyone sprang into action immediately. The sound of automatic weapons fire scattered the tourists in Kranji Countryside, sending them running for the vehicles and tour busses parked along the roadsides, while the farmers sought cover wherever they could find it. In the field behind Shen Wong's barn, a helicopter sailed in over the treetops and landed, with a dozen men exiting it and running towards the house. Another twelve-man team approached down the driveway, completely surrounding the house, and cutting off any possible escape routes.

Within seconds men were scaling the fence surrounding the Wong family residential compound on the outskirts of Singapore City and closing in on the house from all sides.

At WEI-Singapore's regional office in Taipei, Aria's brother and sister were just returning from lunch. When they entered the lobby of the office building, ten men immediately descended upon them, whisking them out of the building and towards an unmarked van waiting at the curbside across the plaza from them.

Brian Ho, the activity monitor that walked Sammy and Jewel out to the parental pickup area saw the van pull up and four strange men jumping out of it. As they approached, he instinctively stepped in front of them, quickly backing them toward the facility doors. Before he could get them to safety, one of the approaching men shot him with a tranquilizer dart, dropping him to the ground as the other men grabbed the children. Danni pulled up to the curbside pickup area less than one minute later, but by then, the children were gone.

The afternoon seemed to drag by for Leung Fu. When the driver called up to his room to notify him that his lawyers and bankers had arrived and were waiting in the lobby, he was floating on a cloud of smugness one could almost smell. His five-thousand-dollar suit seemed to cut through the wind when he walked, and the self-important men gathered around him were drunk on the fumes of power he exuded. After a short ride in a long limousine, Leung Fu and his entourage marched into the AWS office building like victorious generals parading through a village of liberated hostages. The receptionist immediately allowed them access to the corporate elevator which took them directly to the private office of Aria Wong.

On their way up, inside the glass elevator overlooking the bay, he could see the WEI-Singapore office building, reaching into the sky like a modern-day Tower of Babel. For years, he had allowed them to expand and prosper throughout Asia, based on a gentlemen's agreement forced upon him by the impudent Jacob Payne. Now, these two ivory towers stood like sentinels on opposite sides of Marina Bay, taunting Leung Fu like temples paying homage to the upstarts he had failed to crush.

Upon reaching the executive office on the top floor, the elevator opened to a long hallway leading directly to the office door of Aria Wong. He could see her long before he reached her office. She was standing in the doorway holding it open for him as he marched defiantly down the corridor. His thousand-dollar shoes fitted with metal taps, clicked loudly on the Bedrosian marble floors, echoing from the highly polished stone walls and unexpectedly high ceiling overhead. The sound was so ominous that the employees in his Hong Kong office literally cringed upon hearing it, scrambling about like mice in search of holes to hide in.

When he reached her door, he brushed right past her into the office, taking a seat behind the large wooden desk and placing his feet on the highly polished surface while leaning back to make himself comfortable. His entourage followed suit, pushing more of the ornately upholstered chairs closer to the desk and taking their seats in them.

Looking about as if irritated that she had not offered him and his cadre of bankers and lawyers some sort of refreshments, he asked, "Where is your hospitality? Can you not see that these gentlemen need something with which they might quench their thirst?"

"Oh, I am deeply sorry, Mr. Fu," said Aria. "This is the office of my personal assistant's secretary. I've given both of them the afternoon off today, but if you will follow me, my office is right through these doors. I'm sure you will find it much better suited for our meeting."

Leung Fu was visibly irritated at the minor fumble on his part, and quickly stood to follow her through the double doors into the next room. His entourage, visibly flustered by their own impulsive behavior, also rose to follow Mr. Fu like obedient sheep.

As Leung entered the large spacious office, he heard a familiar voice saying, "Good afternoon, Mr. Fu. I'm glad you could make it."

Turning quickly, he was shocked to see none other than the handsome billionaire, Jacob Payne standing directly in front of him. Looking around the long conference table, he saw Danielle Payne with their children, Sammy and Jewel, Aria's grandfather Shen, her parents Michael and Lisa Wong, and Aria's brother and sister, Steven and Cindy Wong from Taipei, Taiwan.

"Thank you so much for joining us," said Aria, closing and locking the door behind her.

CHAPTER 25

PRIOR TO LEAVING Kranji Countryside Wednesday morning, Aria had breakfast with her grandfather. As they were both finishing their coffee, Aria said, "Opa, do you still believe in dragons?"

"Of course," said Shen. "Such majestic creatures do not simply disappear overnight."

"Would you like to see one?" asked Aria with a smile.

"I think so," answered Shen. "I'm just not sure how safe it would be to see one, especially if it also saw me."

"I want to show you something," said Aria, standing up and walking towards the front door. Noticing Shen's perplexed expressions, she said, "Come on, Opa. It's okay. Really."

Shen slowly stood and walked toward her, and the two of them walked out to the barn together. At the Przewalski's horse's stable, she asked, "Would you allow J'Mir to speak with you?"

"Speak with me?" asked Shen. "What do you mean?"

"He cannot speak with you unless you allow him to. Is it okay for him to communicate with you?" reiterated Aria.

"Yes," said Shen, still somewhat curiously.

"Place your hand against his head," said Aria.

Shen slowly placed his hand against the horse's head with his eyes closed. In his mind, he clearly heard J'Mir saying, "Do not be afraid, Mr. Wong. I would never harm you."

Quickly pulling his hand away, Shen stared blankly, first at the horse, then at Aria with his mouth agape. "I... I could hear... He spoke to me." said Shen in barely more than a whisper.

"Yes," said Aria, gently taking Shen's hand and placing it back against J'Mir Mahajan's head. "Don't be afraid. He wants to show you who he really is."

Without a word, Shen allowed J'Mir into his mind again. "I am J'Mir Mahajan, and I am King of the Northeastern Dragon Kingdom, and your granddaughter Aria; she is my bonded rider."

As a smile slowly crossed Shen's face, Aria returned to the house to the absolute oblivion of her grandfather. Shen and King J'Mir Mahajan remained connected for over an hour before he returned to the kitchen where Aria had just finished tidying up the dining room and washing their dishes.

"He is magnificent!" said Shen. "His mind is beautiful, and the way he loves you. Oh, my heavens! He loves you so much!"

"He is my dragon," said Aria. "We are bonded for life, and I love him too. Even when I marry one day and my husband and I have children, my connection to J'Mir will never be severed."

"Nor should it be!" exclaimed Shen. "Any man who cannot see how wonderful that is, doesn't deserve you!"

Aria had never kept secrets from her grandfather, and it was wonderful that she could now share this with him. They spoke for nearly two more hours before Aria had to leave for Singapore City. During that time, she told him that the snow leopard was also a dragon named Mi'Kah D'Monicus, and one of J'Mir Mahajan's most loyal lieutenants. He was there to ensure Shen's safety, and no matter what happened, he could trust Mi'Kah to protect him.

"There will be men coming here today," said Aria. "I have a meeting with Leung Fu at my office this afternoon, and he will attempt to come here and take you to gain leverage over me. I need you to trust me, and trust Mi'Kah. He is a ferocious warrior, and Leung Fu doesn't even *have* enough mercenaries to get past him. Don't worry about the material things here. Those things can all be replaced. J'Mir and I moved all of the animals to a safe location last night, so there is no need to worry over them. You are what is important to me, and Mi'Kah will never allow you to be injured."

Shen nodded intermittently as he listened to all of Aria's instructions. When she finished, she asked, "Do you have any questions, Opa?"

"Only one," said Shen. "Did you say the snow leopard is a dragon too?"

Michael and Lisa Wong had been removed from the residential compound long before sunrise in a vendor's bakery van. The van delivered fresh baked bread to them every morning at 5:00 a.m., and when it left through the main gate, Michael and Lisa were inside it along with the rest of the on-property staff. After they safely reached Aria's corporate office building, the security staff was replaced by Singapore Police Special Operations Command forces during the regular shift change at 7:00 a.m., shortly before sunrise. They had also replaced the security team at WEI-Singapore; another high-priority target in Aria's estimation.

In Taipei, Steven and Cindy Wong had been unreachable. Leung Fu's electronic surveillance agents in Hong Kong had successfully blocked their mobile telecommunications, isolating them in case Aria or one of her family members attempted to warn them. When Leung Fu's men grabbed them in the lobby, they were truly taken by surprise. Suddenly they were being whisked back out the door and escorted across the small plaza in front of the office building. As they approached an unmarked van parked at the edge of the plaza, they were forcefully separated from the men holding onto their arms. The van at the curb unexplainably flattened downward like a stomped paper cup, right before their very eyes. The men in front of them began flying through the air like ragdolls, as if being attacked by a group of angry poltergeists when darkness completely enveloped them. When the darkness dissipated, Steven and Cindy were standing in the lobby of AWS, and what appeared to be an arctic ferret was scampering out through the revolving door and disappearing down the walkway in front of the building.

In Hawaii, Sammy and Jewel were already looking forward to visiting Big Kahuna's Pizza. With Jake being in Singapore to support Aria Wong during her meeting with Leung Fu, Danni agreed to take them to their favorite restaurant for dinner. Neither Aria nor Jake had calculated their abduction into the equation. First of all, it was over five thousand miles from Hong Kong, and nearly seven thousand miles from Singapore. Frankly, Jake was prepared for personal threats and actions taken against him, but he never imagined Leung Fu would be callous enough to kidnap his children. Besides, they were always in the company of a supervising adult, and Brian Ho would do anything in his power to protect them.

After tranquilizing Brian, the kidnappers forced Sammy and Jewel into the back of the van. Once they were inside, three of the men jumped into another trailing vehicle, and the man who shot Brian got into the van and drove them out of the city. The second vehicle followed them for several miles before breaking off when the driver of the van drove down a narrow dirt road to Makua Beach. Sammy sat protectively in front of Jewel, pressing her into the corner behind the driver's seat. When the man opened the sliding side-door, he said, "Get out."

"No!" shouted Sammy. "I want my mom!"

"Your mom isn't coming, but if you get out now, we can call her and she can come here to pick you up," said the man, flashing an obviously fake smile.

"You call her!" exclaimed Jewel. "I can give you her number."

Losing the insincere smile, the man pointed the dart gun at Sammy and said, "If you don't get out right now, I will shoot both of you. We can either do this my way, or we can do it my way."

Looking at each other, Sammy took Jewels hand and slowly exited the van with her. When they were clear of the door, the man raised the dart gun and fired it as Sammy turned to cover Jewel. The dart struck Sammy in the middle of his back, but surprisingly, he didn't even flinch. When he turned to look at the man, his face and skin were covered in glossy black scales, and his eyes were a golden glow. An instant later Jewel released a scream directed at the man. His eyes widened in terror as blood began dripping from his nose, ears, and tear ducts. Behind him, the very fabric of time began to warp, and a black window opened like the mouth of a great white shark. Sammy instantly lunged forward, pushing the man, sending him flying several feet through the air, right into the vortex which immediately closed behind him.

A few seconds later, Danni's car appeared at the top of the rise leading down to the beach. Using the *Helicopter Mom* monitoring chips sewn into their clothing, she was able to track them to their location. She immediately saw the van on the beach and drove toward it, stopping at the edge of the sand. Sammy and Jewel were sitting there as if nothing had happened when she reached them and wrapped her arms around them.

"Oh my god!" she said, exceedingly happy to see them. "I was so worried about you! Are you both alright?"

"We're fine," said Sammy as Jewel nodded silently in agreement.

"Where is the driver?" asked Danni, looking around the dark beach for any sign of him. In the sand, she noticed the dart gun he had used to tranquilize Brian and picked it up while continuing to scan the beach for him. "Where did he go?" asked Danni.

"He shot me with that gun, so Jewel screamed at him and opened the window, and I pushed him into it," said Sammy.

Shocked and in utter disbelief, Danni frantically queried, "What window?" Turning to Jewel, she asked, "Where did you send him, Sweetheart?"

"I only know two windows," said Jewel. "Grandma and Grandpa are probably sleeping, so I sent him to Tikka."

CHAPTER 26

"MIGHT I OFFER YOU AND YOUR ASSOCIATES something to drink?" asked Aria. "The staff will be serving a small late-afternoon meal for us soon, and for dessert, the fresh beignets are absolutely to die for," she added with a genuine smile.

Leung Fu felt as if he were having a mild stroke, and his left eye began to twitch involuntarily. How was this even possible? His people supposedly had eyes on everyone inside this room fewer than three hours ago. The mere fact that they were all here was a physical impossibility. It took nearly five hours to fly from Taipei to Singapore, and a full day to travel there from Hawaii. Despite that indisputable fact, here they all were.

"I think you should have a seat, Mr. Fu," said Aria. "You don't look well. Would you like some water?" she asked, politely.

"How are you all here?" asked Leung Fu, feeling as if he might faint. "My people said,"

"I understand," interrupted Aria. "Our meeting was scheduled for two hours from now, but since you arrived early, and everyone was already here, we decided to accommodate you as best we could."

The lawyers and bankers in his entourage seemed just as perplexed as Leung Fu. In their briefcases and designer satchels, they had prepared contracts in which Aria would be required to sign over full control of her company and the patents for the MRCs to Leung Fu. In return, they would only kill her grandfather, and give her a generous salary of one million dollars per year to continue running the worldwide operations, just as she had run them before Mr. Fu acquired her billion-dollar company. As their eyes nervously darted around Aria's expansive office, it was clear that Mr. Fu was nowhere near having the leverage he had envisioned fewer than three minutes ago. Instead, he looked like a feeble old man who had just completed a half-marathon and finished in last place.

"I am happy to see you've brought your corporate legal team with you," said Aria. "It will save us a lot of time if we can negotiate the contractual agreements and close on everything today. Please, gentlemen. Have a seat," she added without even the slightest hint of sarcasm.

Once everyone had taken their seats around the conference table, a handful of waiters appeared, sliding place settings in front of everyone and filling their drinking glasses before the food servers entered the opulent chamber with a mouthwatering selection of warm gourmet sandwiches.

Despite the obvious tension in the room, everyone seemed to gradually look beyond the circumstances that brought them there as the smell of the delicious banquet before them filled the air. Sitting next to Aria at the head of the table and directly across from Jacob Payne, Leung Fu felt as if he'd entered an alternate reality, with neither of them giving him so much as a dirty look. During the meal, his phone was vibrating nonstop inside his jacket pocket, and after several minutes, he simply turned it off. Regardless of what might transpire after the meal, Leung Fu had no reason to suspect anyone in the room harbored any kind of animosity towards him as they enjoyed their food and drinks.

Once everyone had eaten their fill, and sampled the heavenly beignets Aria had alluded to, the wait staff removed the remaining food and dishes from the table, and Aria thanked everyone for joining her and her esteemed guests for the early dinner, as they filed out of the room.

Once her family members and Danielle Payne had departed with the children, the only people remaining inside the room were Leung Fu and his team, Aria Wong, Jacob Payne, and the ever-present little white chihuahua that appeared to be sleeping on the floor near Jake's chair.

"I wasn't sure whether or not you'd had the opportunity to review this yet, but just to recap, we would like to show you our presentation," said Aria, lowering the lights in the room as monitor screens descended from the ceiling, bathing the room in a warm, blue glow. "Let's begin," she said pressing a button on her remote and bringing the screens to life.

Within seconds, Leung Fu and his team were completely engrossed by the parade of hand-drawn artistic renderings created by Jacob Payne. As the presentation continued, Leung Fu realized just how much of a fool he'd been; not only because of the obvious financial landslide this business would create for his legitimate dealings via his Asian distribution network, but also because of the suffering that Aria Wong's and Jacob Payne's Magnetic Resonance Chambers could end permanently. To make matters worse, this presentation had been on his desk for four days. Had he only taken ten minutes to watch it, the money he'd just wasted on a myriad of failed raids and abduction attempts, could already be curing bacterial and viral infections across all of Asia.

At the end of the presentation, the lights came up slowly and the monitors disappeared into the ceiling recesses overhead. Looking to Leung Fu, Aria asked, "So, Mr. Fu. What do you think?"

After a moment of silence, Mr. Fu rose to his feet and said, "Aria Wong. Jacob Payne. I have severely underestimated both of you, and it is clear that the time has come to change directions and create a new legacy. Despite the many ways in which I have wronged each of you, your willingness to offer me a path to redemption is an act of mercy, I simply do not deserve. Today, I have dishonored myself, attempting to return to the old ways instead of embracing the new. I have been deluded by my own arrogance and undone by sacrificing my honor for unwarranted revenge. The hand of friendship you extended to me, I struck at like a cobra, out of a habit that no longer has a place in this world."

Gesturing around the table, Leung Fu said, "While I will accept your generous offer on behalf of my company, it is not I who will be fulfilling the terms of it. That shall fall to the shoulders of my sons, who have long encouraged me to embrace a new path; a path they embraced many years ago. It is time for younger and wiser men to shape the future of Asia and the world, and once everything has been arranged, perhaps I will seek enlightenment in the solitude of the Himalayas."

"Thank you, Mr. Fu," said Aria. "It would be my honor to work with you, and if Mr. Payne concurs, then we can proceed."

Nodding and rising to his feet, Jake extended his hand across the table to Leung Fu, saying, "I too, would be honored to work with you."

Having reached an accord, Leung Fu's team went to work fine tuning the terms of the agreement. They would be working deep into the night, but by morning, there would be a strong partnership bringing hope to millions of people who, before now, had none.

When Shen Wong arrived at his farm in Kranji Countryside, the scattered wreckage of the Chinese Z-20 helicopter had already been cleared from his pasture, and except for a few broken windows and a damaged front door, the house seemed to have weathered the assault fairly well.

It was late evening when Aria and King J'Mir Mahajan landed quietly in the field behind her grandfather's barn. After Aria went up to the house to join her grandfather, the Przewalski's horse walked out into the pasture where he was soon joined by a Bengal tiger, an Asiatic cheetah, an Arctic fox, a snow leopard, and an Arctic ferret.

"Thank you, my brothers, all," said King J'Mir Mahajan. "Today, you bravely came to the aid of not only my bonded rider and her family, but of the entire Northeastern Dragon Kingdom. T'Pal and Mi'Kael, without you, the livelihood of each of these farmers here in Kranji Countryside would have certainly been lost, and those responsible would have escaped."

T'Pal and Mi'Kael Mahajan had shielded Shen Wong's farm and prevented the assault team from setting the entire community ablaze. Once the mercenaries realized they were facing an unseen foe who had vastly outmaneuvered them, they attempted to retreat to the helicopter, which T'Pal promptly swatted out of the sky into the empty pasture. By the time the Singapore police arrived, all of the assault team's escape vehicles had been unexplainably destroyed, leaving them no choice but to surrender.

"Mi'Kah D'Monicus," said King J'Mir Mahajan. "There are few things more beloved by Aria Wong than her grandfather. You have safeguarded him as if he were your own, and Aria expresses her eternal gratitude for all you've done to protect him."

Once the assault team tossed smoke grenades through the windows of the house, Mi'Kah D'Monicus enveloped Shen Wong and used the same smoke they'd hoped to use in abducting him, to escape with Shen, completely unnoticed by the mercenaries. Within minutes, he'd delivered the elderly man to the rooftop of Aria's office building, having allowed him to experience the thrill of a lifetime, soaring through the sky with a dragon!

"K'Zahn D'Monicus and T'Aru Malka'Am," said King J'Mir Mahajan. "Were it not for you, no one could have reached Steven and Cindy Wong in time to save them. As you have saved the siblings of my bonded rider, so have you also become my brothers."

K'Zahn had been perched on the roof of WEI-Singapore's Taipei regional office while T'Aru located and shadowed Steven and Cindy from the sky. When the van screeched to a halt at the curbside and the driver exited the vehicle to open the side door, K'Zahn leapt from the roof, landing on top of the van, and flattening it into the ground. In the ensuing panic and disarray, T'Aru Malka'Am latched onto the two men holding Aria's brother and sister, flinging them into the granite-clad foundation of the building as K'Zahn swept the rest of them out of the way like fallen leaves. Wrapping his wings around Steven and Cindy Wong, T'Aru Malka'Am simply stepped backwards into Ahl Sha H'Araah, appearing seconds later in the lobby of the AWS corporate office building in Singapore, in the form of his Arctic ferret avatar.

"Each of you have answered my call, and together we have achieved that which none of us could have accomplished alone," said King J'Mir Mahajan. "From this day forward, let there be no shame associated with the D'Monicus bloodline, for as of this very moment and forevermore, you are all my brothers."

As all but J'Mir reverted to their dragon identities beneath a dark night sky, T'Pal Mahajan said, "I now fully understand King T'Aer Bolun Dakkar's mysterious question, and the answer has evolved."

The other dragon warriors turned to face T'Pal as he asked, "If not you, then who?" Turning to face King J'Mir Mahajan, he answered, "If not you... Then all of us!"

It was with great pride that a Przewalski's horse stood alone in the meadow, watching the most valiant dragons in his kingdom, disappear one-by-one into the glistening soul of a billion stars overhead.

CHAPTER 27

THE PORTAL MAPPING SYSTEM created by King NaDahl D'Monicus was not only an essential element of the MRC technology. His painstaking maps of Earth's dimensional portals shed new light on the planet's inter-portal pathways. While all dragons instinctively knew how to enter Ahl Sha H'Araah, they would always leave it within close proximity of their entry point. By providing them with specific portal coordinates, dragons could traverse great distances in a matter of seconds, just as T'Aru Malka'Am had traveled from Taipei to Singapore in the blink of an eye.

After collecting Danni and the children from Makua Beach and taking them to Singapore, he returned to Nin'Jahlah and discovered the missing driver, right where Sammy and Jewel had deposited him. Sitting in the pasture surrounded by four hundred hybrid dinosaurs, he was all but curled into a fetal position sucking his thumb. That condition was further exacerbated when an enormous dragon dropped out of a clear blue sky and landed twenty feet from him.

Jake slid to the ground along T'Aer Bolun Dakkar's lowered wing, himself towering over the terrified and bewildered man. Kneeling in the grass next to the man, Jake looked like a much larger version of the scaly child that had pushed him into this dimension filled with monsters.

"Listen very closely," said Jake. "You will tell no one of this place, and you will never, ever, attempt to kidnap another child, or anyone else for that matter."

Gripping the man firmly enough to leave finger indentations in the Kevlar vest the man was wearing, Jake lifted him from the ground high into the air. With his feet dangling in mid-air, the driver's eyes grew even wider, when T'Aer Bolun Dakkar's massive, clawed hand encircled him and Jake climbed back up the dragon king's lowered wing. Assuming this was the end, the man closed his eyes tightly, expecting his head to be bitten off, as if he were in some Hollywood movie. Instead, he found himself on Makua Beach next to the empty van. Looking down, he discovered he was standing in the giant-sized footprint of the dragon who had brought him back to the scene of his crime.

The assault teams that raided the Wong residential compound and the offices of WEI-Singapore, were met with overwhelming force by the Singapore Police Special Operations teams staged inside both locations. Upon realizing they had stormed right into a trap, the vastly outnumbered mercenaries surrendered immediately without a single shot being fired.

After an exceptionally long day, Jake, Danni, and the kids spent the night in Singapore. Aria Wong had graciously invited them to stay at her private residence inside the AWS corporate office building. The kids had never seen a city like Singapore and were beyond amazed by the view of the Marina Bay Sands Sky Park from the living room window of Aria's executive suite.

Having successfully defined the contours of the Asian Distribution Charter between Payne International, AWS, and Fu Imports and Exports of Hong Kong, Jake and Danni decided to spend the rest of the week in Singapore with Sammy and Jewel. Despite having businesses and corporate partners in nearly every country on Earth, it was a rare occurrence for them to actually make time for a family vacation.

Danni notified the school that Sammy and Jewel were fine, but she and Jake would be keeping the kids out through the weekend, until the buzz surrounding their attempted abduction had died down a bit. After exhaustively touring Singapore City, they took the kids out to Kranji Countryside on the final day of their visit, where Sammy and Jewel seemed to feel right at home, surrounded by baby goats and miniature Falabella horses, and a particularly rare and amazing Przewalski's horse.

"Thank you for your hospitality," said Jake, as he and his delightful family prepared to leave Singapore.

"It was an honor to host you," said Aria. "And Opa loves the twins," she added, watching him follow along behind them as they chased baby goats through the pasture. "You are welcome to bring them here whenever you'd like."

"That is certainly something we will take you up on," said Danni. "It has really been an eye-opening experience for them, and we cannot thank you enough for accommodating us."

"Don't mention it," said Aria. "The pleasure has been all ours."

"You are a brilliant person, Miss Aria Wong," said Jake. "Greatness is your destiny."

"I have excellent mentors," said Aria. "Hopefully, you will not tire of my questions too quickly."

"That is doubtful," said Jake. "However, there is another matter we must attend to soon. King T'Aer Bolun Dakkar has requested the presence of you and King J'Mir Mahajan at his roost in the Line Islands at midnight tomorrow night."

"Then, we shall be there," replied Aria, without hesitation.

After corralling the kids and loading them into their rental vehicle, Jake turned to Shen, saying, "Thank you Shen, for your friendship and generosity. I look forward to our next encounter."

"As do I, Jake," Shen replied. "Be well, my friend."

As Shen and Aria watched them drive down the lane and turn onto the highway, they were both reminded of Jake's last visit; a visit that had changed everything. Without a word, Aria locked her arm into her grandfather's. Leaning her head against his shoulder, the two of them headed back to the house, smiling for the same, yet different reasons.

In Nin'Jahlah, the Payne family was happy to be home again. The pasture filled with horses and goats was replaced with one populated by hybrid dinosaurs, but Sammy's and Jewel's affection for them was no less enthusiastic. The episode on Makua Beach was already long forgotten, and they were actually excited to be returning to school on Monday morning. Their trip to Singapore was an adventure they could actually share with their friends, barring a few obvious redactions, of course. Nevertheless, with a plethora of selfies and cell phone photos to show everyone, it would be easy for them to avoid disclosing their "family secret" and other confidential details of their travels.

Jake and Danni were both quite impressed with Aria Wong and the organization she'd built with little outside guidance. Her passion for helping people and conserving life was on par with Danni's, and the two of them were now formidable advocates for the preservation of Mother Earth.

With trusted bonded riders now representing each of the four dragon kingdoms, Jake and T'Aer Bolun Dakkar were confident the planet was on a sustainable course of environmental recovery. In centuries past, dragons had observed the detrimental actions of human civilizations and their adverse, yet preventable effects. However, without any means of calling attention to them or sharing their knowledge in how to address them, small problems had become progressively larger ones.

Dragons have been Earth's interactive satellites since the beginning of time. From their perspective, high above clouds and storms and atmospheric disturbances, they could see and correctly interpret images and weather patterns as well as recognize the preventable actions which caused them. With bonded riders now capable of communicating those concerns to Earth's human population, their ability to develop timely countermeasures had been markedly enhanced.

Even with the convenience of the portal grid system making it incredibly simple to disappear from one location and reappear in another almost instantaneously, there wasn't a dragon alive who would trade it for the unparalleled experience of flight. The freedom of floating above the planet, suspended between outer space and Earth's inner atmosphere, even for dragons, was the very height of their existence. Crossing vast distances at unimaginable velocities in defiance of gravity itself, offered a level of exhilaration unmatched by anything.

Two nights after returning to Nin'Jahlah, Jake and King T'Aer Bolun Dakkar greeted Aria and King J'Mir Mahajan at his royal roost in the Line Island chain. After their customary greeting, both dragons ascended into the sky on an unerring path at dizzying speed, with J'Mir Mahajan drafted in the wake of the enormous T'Aer Bolun Dakkar. After an intentionally circuitous route from the South Pacific into the northern hemisphere, they plunged like daggers into the heart of the Greenland Sea. Guided by millions of years of instinct more than a fixed trajectory, they were soon navigating their way up from the ocean floor through a maze of ancient volcanic stovepipes and into the ancestral dragon burial grounds of the Northwestern Dragon Kingdom.

As they emerged from the crystalline waters of the lagoon, both Kings T'Aer Bolun Dakkar and J'Mir Mahajan, instinctively illuminated the scales along their necks and heads, bathing the gold-plated chamber in a warm golden-yellow light. Both Jake and Aria dismounted their dragons, and T'Aer Bolun Dakkar disappeared into one of the many recesses surrounding the underwater lagoon.

Having been inside the burial chamber of the Northeastern Dragon Kingdom had in no way prepared Aria for the magnitude and overwhelming majesty of the gilded hall in which they now stood. Even King J'Mir Mahajan seemed shocked at the enormity of it.

Aria was obviously confused. Clearly, King T'Aer Bolun Dakkar was in excellent health, and would remain so for centuries to come.

The King of Kings approached holding two unmarked golden medallions; one large and the other somewhat smaller. Looking first at Jake, who nodded in consent, T'Aer Bolun Dakkar presented the larger of the two medallions to King J'Mir Mahajan, and the smaller one to Aria. Following J'Mir Mahajan's cue after watching him press the medallion into his upper left arm, Aria did the same. The medallions were quickly absorbed into their armor, vanishing without a trace. Continuing to follow his lead, as King J'Mir Mahajan lowered his body to the gold-plated floor of the cave, Aria did also.

Gently placing his massive hands upon the shoulders of both of them, King of Kings T'Aer Bolun Dakkar gave the two warriors his blessing, saying, "These will allow you passage into the realm of any dragon king, for they are forged from the blood of the ancestors of all dragon kings. You will be treated with diplomacy by all dragons and dragon kings from this day forward and forevermore. Use them with discretion and wisdom, for they are now a permanent part of your armor," proclaimed T'Aer Bolun Dakkar. "Now rise and be gone from this sacred place."

Without further discussion, both riders remounted their dragons, immediately disappearing into the lagoon, dousing their glowing scales, and plunging the now empty cavern into absolute darkness. T'Aer Bolun Dakkar led them through the maze of volcanic tubes where they emerged from the secret passageway at the ocean floor. Seconds later, they were breaching the surface of the Greenland Sea, and parting ways as Jake and King T'Aer Bolun Dakkar headed south, and King J'Mir Mahajan set course for Kranji Countryside on the tiny island nation of Singapore.

After landing in the pasture behind Shen Wong's barn, Aria was still somewhat perplexed by the ritual they had just experienced and asked King J'Mir Mahajan, "What prompted King T'Aer Bolun Dakkar to bestow such a significant honor upon us?"

"It resulted from the successful test of your personal integrity," answered King J'Mir Mahajan.

"But I do not recall ever being subjected to such a test," said Aria.

"It is impossible to test an individual's integrity when they are aware, they are being tested," said J'Mir Mahajan. "Your test was conducted by Jacob Payne and King of Kings T'Aer Bolun Dakkar on the evening of our ascension."

"I still do not understand," said Aria. "Of all the experiences during my lifetime, no single event has ever left me with a more confused pairing of sentiments. The near unbearable sadness I felt at the passing of King J'Amal Aidin Kondur, coupled with the enormous elation I felt for you at your ascension to the Throne of the Northeastern Dragon Kingdom, filled me with a paradox of unrequited emotions. Even so, I cannot recall any test of my integrity on that night, or any thereafter."

"The night of my ascension, you were there with me, surrounded by more golden treasure than any one human has ever possessed. The ease with which you could have removed a portion of it was clear and evident, yet you weren't even the least bit tempted to do so. The intoxication of dragon gold has toppled kingdoms and left civilizations in ruin, yet it held no power of enticement over you."

"How could anyone ignore the magnitude of such a moment and succumb to the allure of gold, like some common tomb raider?" asked Aria.

"There are many who could, but you are not one of them," said J'Mir Mahajan. "A person's integrity can only be measured in secret, when their choices are guided by their character, concealed from the scrutiny of others. That night, you unquestionably proved your trustworthiness beyond all doubt."

"But how could they have known?" asked Aria.

"Because they were also there," replied J'Mir Mahajan dispassionately.

"What?" asked Aria, completely taken aback. "Did you know?"

"Of course," replied King J'Mir Mahajan. "I always know when the King of Kings is near."

Smiling quietly to herself, Aria asked, "Had I not asked you, would you have told me?"

"Probably not," replied King J'Mir Mahajan. "I have had faith in you since our first dreamscape encounter, and King T'Aer Bolun Dakkar merely confirmed what I have always known in my heart to be true."

"Hmmm," said Aria, curiously. "Is there anything else I need to know?"

"You need only ask," replied the dragon king.

"But how do I know what to ask?" queried Aria.

"Well, that is something only you can know," said J'Mir Mahajan.

"Why do I get the feeling you are dodging the question?" asked Aria, laughing out loud.

"Is that a 'question' question, or are you just speculating out loud?" replied J'Mir, obviously toying with her.

As their playful banter continued, Shen Wong watched them from the kitchen window with a smile that only seldom a face has borne.

CHAPTER 28

THE MOST VALUABLE COMMODITY, for both humans and dragons, is time. With the possible exception of Fire King J'Akkar, that is the one inescapable truth for all living things on Earth. Since Jake and Danni were teenagers, they had dedicated their lives to protecting those who had no voice, and therefore, no representation. For so long, their focus had been on leaving a better world for their children, than they had inherited from their parents, and by all accounts, they had done an amazing job.

Now that the four dragon kings were working hand-in-hand, with their bonded riders sharing their specialized knowledge and abilities for the good of everyone, Jake and T'Aer Bolun Dakkar unexpectedly had more of that non-renewable resource at their disposal. Suddenly, they had time not only to react to emergencies, but to plan and develop lasting solutions while shoring up the measures they had implemented over years of dogged work and determination. Even though, as King of Dragon Kings, T'Aer Bolun Dakkar's counsel was occasionally sought by each of the ruling dragon kings, with passionate champions like Svend Erickson, Sibyl Dupree, and Aria Wong, they were more than capable of determining and implementing any required course corrections with the full confidence of Jake and T'Aer Bolun Dakkar.

With the luxury of added time for reflection, Jake recognized more and more of himself in Sammy, and could not overlook the fact that Jewel was virtually a carbon copy of the eleven-year-old Danni, who sat two rows up, and two chairs to the right of him in math class.

The unique language the twins developed as toddlers seemed to have expanded, allowing them to communicate not only with one another, but apparently with every other creature in the animal kingdom. Within minutes of arriving at Kranji Countryside, they were so connected to the animals on Shen's farm, that they were visibly disappointed when Jewel and Sammy had to leave, but clearly perked up when Jewel told them that she and Sammy would visit them again soon. The same was true of the abundant wildlife surrounding Grandpa Sam's property. Even beyond the most common farm animals like dogs and cats, cows, goats, pigs, horses, and sheep, both Jewel and Sammy could also clearly communicate with deer, rabbits, squirrels, wild turkeys, owls, and coyotes. Even rattlesnakes like the one that had bitten Sammy, were somehow able to understand them, and in Sammy's estimation, it had only bitten him due to having been unexpectedly roused from its slumber.

In addition to the language skills she and Sammy shared, Jewel was able to emit hypersonic frequencies far above the range of even the most sensitive ears. These frequencies had the same effect on the portals of the interdimensional rift, as the infrasonic frequencies emitted by the MRCs. It was how she could open windows into and out of Ahl Sha H'Araah. While Tikka had been quite tightfisted in doling out location coordinates to Jewel, with time she would learn to navigate them as well and as quickly as Tikka could, eventually surpassing even the scope of King NaDahl D'Monicus.

It was a warm summer night and the sky above Hawaii was clear and peaceful. As Jake and King T'Aer Bolun Dakkar were about to depart on a routine upper-atmospheric patrol flight to measure the numbers and sizes of oceanic food fish in the South Pacific Ocean, Sammy watched in amazement from the front porch. Just as T'Aer Bolun Dakkar was ready to launch, Jake told the dragon king, "Hold on just a moment."

Looking back, T'Aer Bolun Dakkar lowered his wing and Jake gestured for Sammy to join them. Sammy sprang from the porch and sprinted across the pasture. When he drew nearer, the dragon king lightly tapped the boy's shoulder with a single razor-sharp talon, and Sammy's armor immediately deployed, covering him from head to toe. The moment he placed his hand against the dragon's wing, the scales of his armor instantly meshed and released with those of King T'Aer Bolun Dakkar as he swiftly climbed aboard.

Once positioned directly in front of Jake, just ahead of the dragon king's wings, Jake asked, "Are you ready for the most amazing thing you will ever experience?"

Sammy was so excited, he couldn't even speak the words his mind was formulating, so he simply smiled and nodded. In the next instant, King T'Aer Bolun Dakkar launched into the sky, piercing the veil of Ahl Sha H'Araah and expanding his wings against a backdrop of infinite stars. During their ascent, higher and higher into the atmosphere, Sammy felt as if he were exactly where he belonged.

As they glided weightlessly along the edge of the exosphere, Jake said, "Come on Son. Let me show you something unbelievable!"

Rising to his feet, the scales of Jake's armor kept him inseparably attached to the back of the enormous dragon. Following suit, Sammy also stood, and when Jake ran at full speed down the back of the dragon and leapt from its tail into the open arms of the night, so did Sammy! Beneath them, King T'Aer Bolun Dakkar matched their glide path as they drifted silently through the weightless void.

Jake showed Sammy how the slightest contact between his armor and that of T'Aer Bolun Dakkar, created a connection that could not be broken unless he purposely willed it to be so. That night, the three of them spent hours frolicking in the darkness, dipping, and diving and climbing and soaring, all the while performing the most impressive of acrobatic feats, miles above the surface of Mother Earth.

When the blackness of the horizon began ceding to the dark gray of the approaching sunrise, the three of them descended with the speed of a meteorite, streaking through the atmosphere and plunging into the warmth of the South Pacific Ocean without creating so much as an errant ripple. Beneath the surface, King T'Aer Bolun Dakkar devoured an enormous bait ball of Pacific herring in seconds, before ascending and breaching the ocean's surface, once again taking flight into the rapidly lightening sky above.

Chasing the edge of the receding darkness, Jake, Sammy, and King T'Aer Bolun Dakkar matched the speed of Earth's rotation, travelling the circumference of the globe until the border of the never-ending night brought them back to the skies above Hawaii and the welcoming scent of the deep blue South Pacific.

After watching the magnificence of a sunrise that never grows old, King T'Aer Bolun Dakkar slipped gracefully through the interdimensional rift of Ahl Sha H'Araah, appearing seconds later in the sky above Nin'Jahlah. Below them, Danni and Jewel were waving up at them, surrounded by Tikka and their uniquely beautiful tribe of hybrid dinosaurs. Circling slowly, they descended into the midst of their distinctly different, yet oddly comforting family.

As always, King T'Aer Bolun Dakkar's children were anxious to take cover beneath his royal wingspan as they flocked to him with unbridled love and affection.

After kissing Jake to welcome him home, Danni asked Sammy, "So, how was it?"

"It was amazing!" exclaimed Sammy, briefly recounting their nocturnal adventure to Danni before taking Jewel's hand and rushing ahead with her toward the house. As they reverted to their own unique language so Sammy could more accurately explain the excitement of that maiden voyage to his most treasured confidant, Jake and Danni watched and smiled.

"You know he'll want to go with you every time now, right?" said Danni.

"Of course," said Jake, before adding, "One day sooner than we imagine, it'll be me, wanting to go with *him*."

"You have done well, Jacob Payne," said Danni, kissing him again as they continued up the grassy hillside toward the house.

"*We*," Jake replied, correcting her. "*We*, have done well, Danielle Payne."

When they reached the front porch, before going inside, they turned to look back across the awe-inspiring paradise they had called home for nearly sixteen years.

"It never grows old," said Danni, leaning her head against Jake's shoulder and smiling.

"Soon, the twins will be off to college and making their own way in the world beyond the veil," said Jake. "After that, it will be *their* world to conquer instead of ours."

"Well," said Danni. "In the words of **George R.R. Martin**, *'If you want to conquer the world, you best have dragons.'"*

At the base of the hillside, beneath the branches of a prehistoric baobab tree, the King of Dragon Kings, T'Aer Bolun Dakkar, reposed among his adoring pride of hybrid dinosaurs. His rule would last a thousand years, and until his very last heartbeat, he would forever be... Jake's Dragon.

THE END.

RIANO D. MCFARLAND – Author Information

Riano McFarland is an American author and professional entertainer from Las Vegas, Nevada, with an international history.

Born in Germany in 1963, he is both the son of a Retired US Air Force Veteran and an Air Force Veteran himself. After spending 17 years in Europe and achieving notoriety as an international recording artist, he moved to Las Vegas, Nevada in 1999, where he quickly established himself as a successful entertainer. Having literally thousands of successful performances under his belt, *Riano* is a natural when it comes to dealing with and communicating his message to audiences. His sincere smile and easygoing nature quickly put acquaintances at ease with him, allowing him to connect with them on a much deeper personal level—something which contributes substantially to his emotionally riveting style of storytelling. Furthermore, having lived in or visited many of the areas described in his novels, he can connect the readers to those places using factual descriptions and impressions, having personally observed them.

Riano has been writing poetry, essays, short stories, tradeshow editorials, and talent information descriptions for over 40 years, collectively. His style stands apart from many authors in that, while his talent for weaving clues into the very fabric of his stories gives them depth and a sense of credulity, each of his novels are distinctly different from one another. Whether describing the relationship between a loyal dog and his loving owner in **ODIN**, following the development of an introverted boy-genius in **JAKE'S DRAGON**, chronicling the effects of extraterrestrial intelligence on the development and fate of all mankind in **THE ARTIFACT**, or describing the parallels between people and the objects they hold sacred in **I FIX BROKEN THINGS**, *Riano* tactfully draws you into an inescapable web of emotional involvement with each additional chapter and each new character introduced. Added to that, his painstaking research when developing plots and storylines gives his novels substance which can hold up under even the staunchest of reader scrutiny.

Possessing an uncanny flair for building creative tension and suspense within a realistic plot, *Riano* pulls readers into the story as if they were, themselves, always intended to have a starring role in it. Furthermore, by skillfully blending historical fact with elements of fiction *Riano* makes the impossible appear plausible, while his intensely detailed descriptions bring characters and locations vividly into focus.

Although it's certain you'll love the destination to which he'll deliver you, you'll never guess the routes he'll take to get you there, so you may as well just dive in and enjoy the ride which is certain to keep you on the edge of your seat until the very last paragraph!